The crack of gunfire echoed through the night.

"Down! Get down!" Garrett yelled. He held the infant carrier behind his back with one hand and fired toward the shadow of a man crouched near one of the parked cars.

He missed, the bullet pinging off the side of the vehicle. Garrett hoped the gunfire would bring backup, but the parking lot remained quiet.

Too quiet.

Had the gunman left? No, he didn't think so.

Another crack of gunfire confirmed his suspicion. Garrett placed himself between Liz and Micah as he returned fire. He had no idea who had come after his son.

Crouched behind Garrett, Liz had bent over Micah's infant carrier, protecting the baby with her body.

What in the world was going on? How had the gunman who'd shot Micah's mother known to come here?

And why would anyone want to hurt an innocent baby?

Laura Scott has always loved romance and read faith-based books by Grace Livingston Hill in her teenage years. She's thrilled to have been given the opportunity to retire from thirty-eight years of nursing to become a full-time author. Laura has published over thirty books for Love Inspired Suspense. She has two adult children and lives in Milwaukee, Wisconsin, with her husband of thirty-five years. Please visit Laura at laurascottbooks.com, as she loves to hear from her readers.

Books by Laura Scott

Love Inspired Suspense

Hiding in Plain Sight
Amish Holiday Vendetta
Deadly Amish Abduction
Tracked Through the Woods
Kidnapping Cold Case
Guarding His Secret Son

Justice Seekers

Soldier's Christmas Secrets
Guarded by the Soldier
Wyoming Mountain Escape
Hiding His Holiday Witness
Rocky Mountain Standoff
Fugitive Hunt

Mountain Country K-9 Unit

Baby Protection Mission

Visit the Author Profile page at LoveInspired.com for more titles.

Guarding His
Secret Son

LAURA SCOTT

LOVE INSPIRED SUSPENSE
INSPIRATIONAL ROMANCE

LOVE INSPIRED® SUSPENSE
INSPIRATIONAL ROMANCE

ISBN-13. 978-1-335-98002-1

Guarding His Secret Son

Recycling programs for this product may not exist in your area.

For questions and comments about the quality of this book, please contact us at CustomerService@Harlequin.com.

® is a trademark of Harlequin Enterprises ULC.

Love Inspired
22 Adelaide St. West, 41st Floor
Toronto, Ontario M5H 4E3, Canada
www.LoveInspired.com

Printed in Lithuania

MIX
Paper | Supporting responsible forestry
FSC® C021394

But Jesus called them unto him, and said, Suffer little children to come unto me, and forbid them not: for of such is the kingdom of God. Verily I say unto you, Whosoever shall not receive the kingdom of God as a little child shall in no wise enter therein.
—*Luke* 18:16–17

This book is dedicated to all the
wonderful midwives taking care of pregnant moms.
You are a blessing to so many.

ONE

"Please save my baby!"

Midwife Liz Templeton was doing her best to do just that. This stranger, Rebecca, had shown up at her clinic in Liberty, Wisconsin, with a bullet lodged in her chest and in full-blown labor. Liz had placed a pressure dressing over the bullet wound before turning her attention to the baby.

"Easy now, I see this little guy's head." Liz kept her tone reassuring. She'd had many unusual cases arrive on her doorstep, but a pregnant woman in labor suffering a gunshot wound was a first. "With the next contraction, you need to push."

"Okay." Rebecca panted, a layer of sweat over her brow. Her face was so pale because of the pain and the blood loss from her injury.

"It would be better if I could call 911," Liz repeated for the second time.

"No! Please don't. He'll find and kill me. Please!"

There wasn't time to ask questions about who "he" was and why he'd shot her. Not when the baby's birth was imminent.

"Push," Liz said. "Come on, Rebecca, push!"

Her wounded patient did her best, bearing down with the

contraction. But Rebecca was weak, and the baby's head didn't breach the birth canal.

"Harder! Push harder!" Liz ordered.

With a low groan, Rebecca tried again, putting all her effort into the push. This time, Liz was able to gently guide the baby's head toward her. She quickly cleared the infant's nose and mouth with a bulb suction and towel.

"Good job. He's almost here. Come on, Rebecca, you can do it!"

Tears streaked down Rebecca's cheeks as she panted, waiting for the next contraction. Then she gave another push, and the baby was born.

"You did it!" Liz wrapped the baby in the towel, then clamped the umbilical cord. The little guy cried, showing off a nice set of lungs. Once she'd snipped the cord, she brought the crying baby up to Rebecca. "Isn't he beautiful? Meet your son."

"Yes. Micah. Beaut…" Rebecca's eyes drifted shut.

"Rebecca?" Panic seized Liz by the throat. She turned and placed the wrapped newborn in the warmer, then rushed to her patient. "Look at me, Rebecca. Open your eyes!"

The injured woman opened them just enough to look at her. "Take Micah to Deputy Garrett Nichols." Rebecca's tone was barely more than a whisper. "Tell him—keep his son safe."

Liz didn't understand. She peeked beneath the gauze over Rebecca's chest wound, horrified to see the right side of her chest blowing up like a balloon. The tension pneumothorax must have happened when she'd pushed to deliver the baby. "Who shot you, Rebecca. Garrett?"

"No!" Rebecca's eyes shot open, meeting her gaze. "Promise me. Take Micah to Garrett! He'll keep Micah safe…"

"I will." Ignoring the crying baby, Liz took a large needle and quickly inserted it between the fourth and fifth ribs along the right side of Rebecca's chest. If she didn't relieve the tension of the pneumothorax, the pressure would eventually stop Rebecca's heart. A whooshing sound indicated the air had been released, but then blood began pouring out of the opening.

No! Too much blood! Liz was losing her!

She needed to call 911. Unfortunately, her clinic was near the southernmost tip of the Oneida Native American reservation in the middle of nowhere. The closest hospital was eighteen miles away. She quickly made the call, requesting an ambulance, then turned toward the baby.

"Hey, Micah, it's okay." She gathered the baby close, knowing how important skin-to-skin contact was. She couldn't hold him for long, though, and quickly wrapped him in a soft blanket and set him in the warmer. She hurried back to her patient.

"Come on, Rebecca, stay with me." Liz attempted to start an IV, but her veins were already collapsed from blood loss. Desperate, she inserted an intraosseous needle to inject fluids directly into Rebecca's femur. It seemed barbaric, but it was her patient's only chance.

Liz opened the clamp so that the fluids ran wide open. Whispering words of comfort to the baby, she checked Rebecca's vital signs. The new mom's skin was pale and cold. Too cold. Her muscles went slack beneath Liz's fingers; her head lolled to the side.

No, no, no! Liz checked for a pulse.

Nothing.

She pulled a stool over and jumped up to start CPR. She placed her hands on Rebecca's chest and began giving compressions. That's when she noticed that with every push downward, the pool of blood on the floor grew larger.

The bullet must have nicked an artery. After one round of compressions, she felt for a pulse.

Still nothing.

Stifling a sob, she did another round, then another. But then she stepped off the stool. It was no use. CPR wouldn't help if there wasn't blood to circulate through Rebecca's body. She didn't have the luxury of packed red blood cells available in the clinic, and that was the only thing that would save Rebecca now. That, and surgery to repair the torn artery.

Bowing her head to offer a quick prayer, she mentally kicked herself for not calling 911 sooner. She should have anticipated the extensive internal bleeding. Her expertise was childbirth, not traumatic gunshot wounds! But the baby had already been crowning, so that was where she'd focused her efforts.

Now it was too late.

But not for Micah. Rebecca had been shot. Why, Liz had no idea. She hurried back to the warmer. She quickly checked Micah's height and weight, satisfied to note he was seven pounds, five ounces. She took a moment to wash Rebecca's blood from her hands, then used a soft washcloth to bathe Micah. After dressing him in a diaper and a blue onesie, she wrapped him in a clean blanket and carried him with her to her small living area adjacent to the clinic.

Thankfully, she kept a stock of supplies for her low-income mothers, including diapers, infant formula and bottles. Moving through the kitchen, she packed the items in a large diaper bag. As an afterthought, she tossed in the small stuffed bunny she'd bought all those years ago for her daughter. Then she crossed over to the computer she used for her notes. The reservation had internet access, although it wasn't great.

Shifting Micah to one arm, she single-handedly typed *Deputy Garrett Nichols* into the search engine. She got an instant hit. Chief Deputy Garrett Nichols worked for the Green Lake County Sheriff's Department. Discovering he was a cop was reassuring.

Green Lake was sixty miles from her clinic. What had Rebecca been doing here near the rez? Why hadn't she gone to Green Lake, if that's where Micah's father was? Liz hesitated, gazing down at Micah. He'd stopped crying now, having fallen asleep against her. Was she really going to do this? Normal protocol would be to call the Department of Health and Human Services, who would put the baby in foster care.

But Garrett Nichols was the baby's father. He deserved a chance to see his son. Leaving Rebecca behind didn't sit well. Maybe she should wait for the ambulance to arrive. Then she remembered the bullet in Rebecca's chest. No, she couldn't take the risk. If there was any remote possibility the baby was in danger, the best thing she could do was take him to Deputy Garrett Nichols, as his mother had asked—no, had *begged*.

Besides, dropping a baby off at a police station was allowed and protected under the Safe Haven Act. That might still be a stretch, though, because Liz wasn't Micah's mother.

For a moment, the memory of her stillborn daughter flashed in her mind. The ache was always there, a constant reminder of what she'd lost.

Willow was gone, but Micah needed her now.

She would not fail this innocent baby the way she'd failed her own daughter.

Garrett looked up from his desk when Sheriff Liam Harland rapped on the door. His boss's expression was full of concern. "Go home, Garrett."

"I will." He tried to smile, but it wasn't easy. The last ten months had been tough. The day he'd lost a fellow officer in a drug bust, he'd also lost his zest for life.

And his faith.

"I mean it, Garrett." Liam's scowl deepened. "You're not to blame for Jason's death."

He was, but Liam was too nice to say it. Avoiding the topic, Garrett gestured at the computer. "I'm almost finished. I'll be out of here soon."

Liam sighed, obviously not believing him. "If I hear that you slept here in the office again, I'm going to put you on a leave of absence. Understand?"

He winced and nodded. "Yeah, sure. I hear you."

Mumbling something about a bullheaded cop, Liam turned away. Garrett waited until he heard the door of the sheriff's department headquarters close before dropping his head in his hands.

The last thing he wanted was a leave of absence. Yet he also knew he was walking a very fine line. If he didn't pull himself together soon, he'd be no good to the other deputies they had working for them.

Their newest deputies on the team, Wyatt and Abby Kane, were doing great. As soon as they hired a replacement for Jason—no easy task these days, as rural cops were hard to find—he planned to submit his resignation.

Liam would try to talk him out of it, but he'd insist. The team would be better off without him. Wyatt had been an FBI agent and would be a great replacement as chief deputy. Besides, Garrett wasn't sure he had it in him to continue his career. If only he'd gotten to the scene soon enough to save Jason…

But he hadn't. The young officer, barely twenty-five years old, had died. Because he'd been too late.

Stop it, he told himself sternly. They were still short-staffed. That meant he had a job to do.

A loud banging on the front door made him frown. He rose from his desk and strode across the open desk area. Since it was summer, their peak season, he had all deputies out on patrol, leaving him to man the headquarters alone.

His eyebrows levered up in surprise when he saw a pretty woman with long, straight dark hair, pounding on the door. She wore bloodstained scrubs, which puzzled him. Then his gaze dropped to the baby carrier on the ground beside her.

"Deputy Nichols!" She pounded again. "I need to speak to Chief Deputy Garrett Nichols!"

Garrett unlocked and opened the door. He might have expected to see Rebecca, if not for the fact that she'd told him to leave her alone. Honoring her wishes, he'd stopped calling, but he had wondered if she'd just show up out of the blue again, the way she had ten months ago.

The woman standing there was a complete stranger. Someone he'd never seen before in his life.

"I'm Deputy Nichols." He gave her a stern look. "Who are you? Is there danger? Do you need police protection?"

"Oh, I'm so glad it's you!" The dark-haired woman turned and picked up the baby carrier. "May I come inside? I— Yes, need police protection, but this may take a while to explain."

He had no idea what she was talking about, but he opened the door in a silent invitation. She hurried through, just as the baby began to wail.

"Oh, dear, Micah may need to be fed." She looked a bit flustered. "Is there a place we can talk while I give him a bottle?"

"My office." He'd heard of police departments finding babies on their doorstep, but in his ten-year tenure here in Green Lake, that had never happened. The way this woman attended to the baby, though, didn't give him the impression this was a Safe Haven situation.

"Thanks." The dark-haired woman set the baby carrier on his desk, then rummaged through the diaper bag. "I need this filled with warm water. Not too hot," she cautioned. "And only to the line, okay? The formula is in there, so you need to shake it to make sure it dissolves."

"Who are you?" he asked again, taking the bottle from her fingers.

"Liz Templeton." She glanced down at her bloodstained scrubs with a grimace. "Sorry to show up like this. I'm a midwife for the Oneida Native American reservation."

That explained her Native American looks. Straight black hair and light brown skin, but her bright green eyes indicated she had non–Native American blood in her veins, too.

Curious about why she was here, he took the bottle and filled it with warm water, knowing a bit about the process from watching Liam and Shanna take care of their daughter, Ciara.

When he returned to the office, Liz had the baby in her arms. "Thanks so much." She plucked the bottle from his fingers and gave it to the baby.

Watching her, he propped his hip on the edge of his desk, trying to put the puzzle pieces together. Had she delivered this baby? If so, where was the infant's mother? "Why are you here?"

"To find you." She looked up at him, her gaze intense. "Sorry, I should start at the beginning. Do you know a woman named Rebecca?"

Hearing the name of the woman he'd once loved was a sucker punch to the gut. "Yes."

"She gave birth to Micah in my clinic, then told me to

bring him to you. His father. Because you would keep him safe."

Micah? *His* child? The realization hit him like a ton of bricks. He'd spent the night of Jason's death with Rebecca, allowing their close friendship to go too far. He'd always cared for her, even loved her, but when he'd awoken the next day, she was gone. He'd called, and she assured him that as much as she cared for him, too, she didn't love him the way he deserved to be loved. He'd known then, she'd only come to stay in Green Lake as a temporary refuge. Not a permanent move. Especially when she informed him that she was heading back to Chicago, and that he needed to let her go to live his own life.

They'd always been close friends, having met as kids during summer vacations in Green Lake. He'd loved her but had known their relationship wouldn't go anywhere. Which only made his actions the night he'd lost Jason more despicable. He shouldn't have taken advantage of Rebecca's sweetness, her caring. And what he'd thought was her love.

But he had. And now?

"Are you saying Micah is mine?" He pushed the words through his tight throat. This couldn't be happening. Why hadn't Rebecca called him? Warned him? Told him they were going to have a child? "Where is Rebecca now? Why do you have the baby?"

Liz's expression filled with compassion. "I'm sorry, Deputy, but Rebecca died of a bullet wound to the chest minutes after I delivered Micah. I tried to save her, but she lost too much blood, and I don't store blood products in my clinic."

A bullet wound to the chest? He shook his head, grappling with the news. "I don't understand. Who shot her?"

"I don't know." Liz glanced back down at the baby in her

arms. "She couldn't tell me much, other than to bring the baby to you so you would keep him safe."

"'Safe'? From the perp who shot her?"

"I assume so." Liz took the bottle from the baby's mouth and turned to rest him upright on her shoulder. She smoothed her hand in circles along the baby's back. "I was hoping you would know more."

"I don't." None of it made any sense. Rebecca knew he was a deputy; why wouldn't she have come to him sooner if she was in danger? He began to doubt this woman's story. "Why would Rebecca show up at your clinic with a gunshot wound?"

"Good question." She turned the baby back in her arms, gazing down at his sleeping face for a long moment before she looked up at him. "I wish I could tell you more, but honestly, her arrival was a complete shock. Most of my clients are poor, either from the reservation or referred to me because of the free services I provide. Rebecca was dressed in top-notch maternity clothes. She'd had her hair done and beautifully painted nails. Not like my usual clientele."

Yeah, that sounded like Rebecca.

"I've never had a pregnant woman suffering a gunshot wound show up like that," Liz continued. "But on my way here, I saw a Cadillac along the side of the road, about two miles from my clinic. I didn't stop to investigate because I was too scared to risk placing Micah in harm's way."

"We'll go there now." He stood. "I need you to show me the way."

"My clinic is sixty miles from here," she warned. "Although I do have to go home that way, I guess." She rose to her feet and offered the baby. "Don't you want to hold your son?"

His son. Garrett felt as if he'd been jettisoned into outer

space. Was he dreaming? As Liz gently pressed the baby into his arms, he knew he wasn't.

"Micah," he whispered, his heart squeezing in his chest. Ten minutes ago, he hadn't known about his son.

Now he found himself wondering what he was going to do with a new baby. This— He wasn't prepared for this!

"I can give you some of my supplies until you can shop for your own things," Liz said, as if reading his mind.

Her offer was another punch to the gut. He didn't have anything at his place for taking care of a baby. And he didn't have a clue what that all entailed.

"Please take him." He couldn't hide the desperation in his tone as he placed Micah back in her arms. "Let's go. I need to see Rebecca's car. There must be some explanation for what happened. A clue of some sort, to figure out what she meant by keeping Micah safe."

"Okay." She gave him an odd look but didn't argue. He took a moment to shut down his computer, then waited for her to secure Micah in his infant car seat. He noticed a small white stuffed bunny was tucked next to the baby. When she finished, she slung the diaper bag over her shoulder.

When he reached for the handle of the baby carrier, she smiled in approval. He didn't have the heart to tell her that he'd only done that because he knew how heavy it was.

Not because Micah was his son.

His. Son.

There was no reason to believe Liz was lying to him. Why would she? But the entire situation sounded too bizarre to be real.

He was having trouble wrapping his head around the fact that the night Rebecca had comforted him after Jason's death had resulted in her giving birth to a son. *His* son. Without her telling him. That was the part he really struggled with.

"Are you sure Rebecca said the baby was mine?" He held the door open for Liz, then took a moment to lock it behind him. "Maybe she just wanted me to keep him safe."

"I'm positive she said you were Micah's father." There was no hesitation in her statement.

"What else did she say?" He led the way around the building to the parking lot. The hour was past eight, and despite the warm July breeze, the sun had dropped below the horizon.

"She begged me not to call 911 because 'he' would find her and kill her." Liz's voice dropped to a whisper. "She was deathly afraid, Deputy Nichols. And the baby was already crowning, so I placed a pressure dressing over the gunshot wound, then quickly attended to the delivery. But I underestimated how much damage the bullet had caused. There was far too much bleeding into her chest cavity." Her stricken gaze met his. "I— It was horrible. I'm so sorry. Maybe if I had called 911 right away, she'd still be alive."

"I don't blame you, Liz." He could only imagine what she'd been through. "I'm sure that was a very difficult situation to be in."

"One of the worst," she admitted softly.

They had crossed the parking lot and were heading toward a small blue sedan he assumed was Liz's car when the sound of a shoe scraping along the asphalt reached his ears.

Garrett whirled around, reaching for his gun. Holding on to the baby's carrier slowed him down, and he was a second too late.

The crack of gunfire echoed through the night.

"Down! Get down!" He awkwardly held the carrier behind his back with one hand as he aimed and fired toward the shadow of a man crouched near one of the parked cars.

He missed, the bullet pinging off the side of the vehicle. Garrett hoped the gunfire would bring backup, but the parking lot remained quiet.

Too quiet.

Had the gunman left? No, he didn't think so.

Another crack of gunfire confirmed his suspicion. Garrett placed himself between Liz and Micah as he returned fire.

The sound of running footsteps made him think backup had arrived. Then he saw the shadow of a man disappearing down the street. Every cell in his body wanted to give chase, but he didn't dare leave Liz and Micah unprotected.

Apparently, Rebecca was right: Micah was in danger.

Too bad he had no idea who had come after his son.

TWO

Crouched behind Garrett, Liz had bent over Micah's carrier, protecting the baby with her body. Her heart thundered in her chest as gunfire reverberated around them.

What in the world was going on? How had the gunman who'd shot Rebecca known to come here, to Green Lake?

And why would anyone want to hurt an innocent baby?

"We're getting into my SUV, understand?" Garrett's voice was clipped.

She tentatively lifted her head to look around. "Is he gone?"

"I think so." Garrett's grave expression could have been carved from stone. "I'll need you to carry the baby so I can protect us if needed."

The baby? Not *his son?* She frowned but did as he asked since she appreciated the fact that he'd needed his hands free. Seeing him holding the gun made her shiver.

Someone had shot at them! Being square in the middle of gunfire was difficult to comprehend. She straightened and picked up the carrier. Garrett urged her to step in front of him, guiding her to a black SUV not far from her sedan.

He unlocked the vehicle, then stood behind her as she secured the baby carrier, placing it in the car seat so the baby was facing backward. Then she set the diaper bag on the floor.

Garrett escorted her to the passenger seat, again protecting her with his body. Only once she was settled did he jog around to slide behind the wheel. Moments later, he quickly drove out of the parking lot.

"Where are we going?" She didn't like leaving her sedan behind. "I need my car to get back to my clinic. I also use my vehicle to visit patients on the rez." A horrible thought struck her. "Deputy Nichols? Do you think the gunman followed me here to Green Lake?"

"Call me Garrett." He grimaced. "The perp may have followed you, but I don't understand why he would wait to come after you and Micah outside our headquarters. Shooting at us near a police station wasn't smart. Especially when he could have taken you both out on some section of deserted highway, where you wouldn't be easily found."

A chill snaked down her spine. "Thanks for that image."

"Sorry." He patted her hand. "I didn't mean to sound callous, but I do think it's odd the gunman attempted to shoot you here, right next to the sheriff's department headquarters. And his aim was bad, too. The bullet only missed me by inches but didn't come anywhere close to you or Micah."

She frowned, not liking the idea of either of them being a target. Would the gunman kill her just because she'd delivered Micah? That didn't seem logical. Then again, nothing about this situation made sense. "Okay, so where are we going?"

"My place." He shot her a sideways glance. "Don't worry, you and the baby will be safe there."

Rubbing her temple, she strove to remain calm. Being targeted by gunfire had been terrifying. Garrett's place would be safe, but she couldn't just stay in Green Lake indefinitely. She had patients to care for.

Granted, not that many. The rez population had dwindled over the years, especially women of childbearing age. Young people didn't stay on the reservation; they went out to make their way in the world. Still, she was determined to offer her services to pregnant women in need. Pregnant women of any background—Native American, African American, Hispanic or Caucasian. She welcomed them all.

Thankfully, word of mouth—especially from the Green Bay and Appleton areas—had helped bring women to her clinic. Each time she assisted in bringing a new child into the world, her burden felt a little lighter.

Her clinic was partially subsidized by the government, and by the reservation, but she barely made enough money to pay her meager bills. Liz didn't mind. Tending to pregnant women was her calling. And it helped her deal with her own loss.

She was so encompassed with her thoughts that she hadn't realized Garrett had pulled into the driveway of a log home, one that blended nicely against a wooded backdrop. Glancing back at the baby, she wondered if Garrett planned to keep and raise his son. Or if the little boy would end up in foster care.

It bothered her to think Garrett wouldn't keep Micah. She pushed out of the passenger seat, then went around to unbuckle the baby carrier.

Garrett stood, sweeping his gaze around the area as she shouldered the diaper bag and then lifted the carrier out of the car. After a moment's hesitation, he took the heavy carrier from her hand.

The baby continued to sleep as he unlocked the door and pushed it open. Liz stepped over the threshold, greeted by the welcome scent of pine cleaner. The open-concept kitchen and living room were spotlessly clean. He was either a neat freak or had a cleaning service.

After setting the baby carrier on the kitchen table, he turned to look at her. "I have two guest rooms, but no crib or anything like that." He shifted from one foot to the other. "I wasn't expecting this. Rebecca never told me she was pregnant."

"I'm sorry to hear that." She couldn't help but wonder if Rebecca's secret had resulted in her being shot. "Micah can sleep in the carrier for now, although a cradle would be better." She sighed and crossed her arms over her chest. It was late, going on nine o'clock. Getting back to Liberty would take an hour. "We're not going to be here that long, are we?"

"Depends on what the deputies find." He stared down at the sleeping baby for a long moment, then pulled out his cell phone. "Excuse me while I make a few calls. Please make yourself at home."

At home? She found the log cabin beautiful and cozy, but she wasn't comfortable in this level of luxury.

A cot and a small kitchen attached to the clinic was her home.

Micah woke up and began to cry, interrupting her thoughts. Garrett moved farther away from the baby while still on the phone. Liz quickly unbuckled the baby and lifted him into her arms.

"Shh, little one. It's okay. You're fine." She cradled the baby close, holding his head against the V in her neckline to enhance skin-to-skin contact.

He snuggled against her, melting her heart. She would do whatever was necessary to keep the child safe.

Should she take him to the closest hospital? Hand him over to a social worker who could take care of getting him placed in foster care? That may be the safest approach.

"Thanks, Wyatt." Having ended his call, Garrett returned to the kitchen as he pocketed his phone. He seemed confused as to why she was standing there. "Do you need something?"

She stared at him for a long moment. "Do you have any intention of keeping your son?"

His eyes widened as if she'd slapped him, and he took a step back. "I—uh, yeah. I just don't have much experience with babies."

"You won't learn if you refuse to hold him." She walked toward him, pinning him with a narrow gaze. "Take your son, Garrett. He needs to find comfort in your arms, too."

"I— Okay." He took the baby from her arms and cradled him to his chest, much the way she had. The infant rested against him, falling back to sleep within seconds.

"You need to bond with him," she said in a low voice. "He's already lost his mother. He can't lose his father, too."

A pained expression crossed his features. "How am I going to raise a baby? I can't stay home with him twenty-four seven."

She curled her fingers into fists, trying not to lash out at him. A baby wasn't a nuisance. She would have given anything to have Willow alive and in her arms. "Babies are a gift from God, Garrett. If you don't keep him, he'll end up in foster care. Is that what you want?"

"No, but..." His voice trailed off.

She squelched a flash of annoyance. "I'm sure you can get a leave of absence from work until you can make child-care arrangements."

He nodded slowly. "Yes, I can do that." He sounded more sure of himself now. "But I still need to understand the source of the danger." He met her gaze head-on. "And for that, I need your help."

Her help? She wanted to flat-out refuse, but the way

Micah slept against Garrett's shoulder gave her pause. He obviously couldn't fight a gunman with a baby in his arms.

Didn't she owe this much to Rebecca? The woman whose life she'd failed to save?

Yes. Because if something terrible happened to Micah, she would never forgive herself.

Garrett needed to get to work, try to figure out what Rebecca had gotten herself tangled up in—but he couldn't tear his gaze from his son.

At one time, he would have thought God was sending him a clear message, but he wasn't exactly on speaking terms with Him at the moment.

God should never have let Jason die. The twenty-five-year-old officer had been on the force for just over three years.

He'd been so young. Too young to die. If only he hadn't sent Jason to the scene first. If only he'd gotten there sooner. If only...

Garrett gave himself a mental shake. He couldn't afford to wallow in a pool of self-pity. Not over Jason's death or the unexpected arrival of his son.

Liz was right about one thing: babies were a precious gift. He hadn't known about Micah—or why Rebecca had kept the news a secret—but as the baby slept with his face pressed into the side of his neck, he was struck by an unexpected wave of love.

"Rebecca named him Micah?"

"Yes." Liz gestured to the diaper bag. "I have birth certificate forms that need to be filled out. Rebecca didn't give me her last name, and I didn't see a purse or ID when she staggered into the clinic, either. Since she didn't give Micah a middle name, you can choose that one."

Birth certificate. He swallowed hard and nodded. "I'd

like to name him Micah John Nichols. John is my middle name."

"That sounds perfect." She dug inside the bag and pulled out the paperwork.

Somehow, documenting the information on legal forms made it all the more real. There were so many things he'd need to do—to buy—but that would have to wait.

His phone rang. Holding Micah to his chest with one hand, he pulled out the device with the other. After seeing Wyatt's name on the screen, he answered quickly. "Wyatt? Please tell me you found the shooter."

"Sorry, boss, not yet. We have all deputies on alert, though. We scoured the parking lot and found a slug imbedded in the front of a blue sedan. We also found several shell casings. One looks to be from your gun."

"It probably is." He glanced at Liz. "What caliber is the other shell casing from?"

"A .45. We're getting it tested for possible fingerprints."

Garrett knew better than to count on the shooter making a rookie mistake. "Is the blue sedan drivable?"

Liz snapped her head up to look at him, her eyes wide. "My car?" she whispered.

He nodded.

"I'm afraid not. One bullet struck the radiator. There may be other engine damage, too. I'm no expert."

"Okay, do me a favor and call the garage. Have the sedan towed there to be repaired. I'll pay for the damage." He watched Liz sink into the closest kitchen chair as if devastated by the news. And really, he couldn't blame her. None of this was her fault. All she'd done was help deliver a baby.

"Will do. Anything else, boss?" Wyatt asked.

"Just keep an eye out for the shooter."

"We will—but keep in mind that finding someone who

looks out of place among the crush of tourists roaming around will be impossible."

"I know." Their small department was over taxed during the peak tourist season, when those who came to visit their beautiful lakes often misbehaved. It was the main reason he'd intended to wait until fall to quit.

Now that he had Micah to consider, he realized that re-signing from his position was no longer an option. How had his life gotten so complicated, so fast? "Just do your best."

"Sure thing, boss."

Garrett slipped the phone into his pocket and walked over to where Liz sat, her head bowed. "I'm sorry about your car, but I'm sure the repairs will be completed soon."

"I would offer to pay, but I honestly don't have the money for that." She lifted her head, her bright green eyes meeting his. "I should let my insurance company know. They'll cover the repairs above my thousand-dollar deductible."

"Don't worry about that now." He wanted to hand Micah over to her but feared she'd lecture him again. "I need to start investigating Rebecca's murder." He hesitated, then added, "Her father needs to know about her death, too."

"You want me to help take care of Micah while you do those things." She made it a statement, not a question.

"Give me at least twenty-four hours." It was a stretch to think he'd have the investigation completed that quickly. "Can we leave a message for your patients? Some way to let them know you won't be in?"

She nodded. "I left a note on my door saying I would be back in the morning. We'll need to go there sooner or later to check out Rebecca's car, right?" When he nodded, she added, "I'll update the note then."

"Thank you." He owed Liz a huge debt of gratitude. "I'm sorry to drag you into this."

She offered a wan smile. "Rebecca is the one who pulled me into this, not you." When Micah began to whimper, she held out her hands. "I'll take him. He may need to be changed, and I can try feeding him again. Newborns don't eat much, but every little bit is helpful."

He pressed a kiss on the top of Micah's head, then handed him over. "I have a lot to learn."

"Oh, trust me—" she stood and poked through the diaper bag for the supplies she needed "—all new parents feel the same way."

Leaving Liz to it, he crossed over to the small desk he used as a home office. After opening his laptop, he began a search on Rebecca Woodward's name.

Since she was the daughter of Robert Woodward, a real estate mogul in Chicago, Garrett wasn't surprised when dozens of links popped up. With a sigh, he realized going through the numerous articles would take time.

He could hear Liz cooing at Micah as she changed him. Diaper changes were another task he'd need to learn, but not right this minute.

Garrett took a minute to pull up a map of the Oneida Native American reservation. The town of Liberty was right on the border of the southernmost tip of the reservation.

Then he frowned, realizing Rebecca had gone much farther north than she needed to—if she was, in fact, heading to Green Lake to seek his assistance. Not to mention, the many hospitals she'd passed along the way.

If she'd been in labor, the way Liz had described, why not go to the closest ER?

Liz's words echoed in his mind: *She begged me not to call 911 because he would find her and kill her.*

He, who? The gunman, obviously—but why?

Garrett clicked on the first article, from the online newspaper *Windy City Chicago*.

The headline was not what he'd expected: "Robert Woodward Diagnosed with Pancreatic Cancer."

With a frown, he quickly scanned the article. Rebecca was quoted as saying her father was receiving excellent medical care while fighting his stage four pancreatic cancer diagnosis.

Interesting, but not exactly a reason for Rebecca to have been shot and killed.

The baby cried louder now, causing him to glance over to see Liz making a bottle. He jumped up and went over to help.

"Take the baby," she said as she ran the water, waiting for it to warm up. "I'll be ready in a minute."

He picked up Micah, bemused by his loud crying. "Do all newborns have lungs like this?"

She froze, then nodded. "Most do, yes."

He sensed he'd hit a nerve, but he didn't push. He walked with the baby, pacing back and forth as she made the bottle. When she'd finished, she headed into the living room. He followed, giving her a moment to get settled on the sofa before handing Micah back to her.

"Forgive me for asking, but the name Templeton doesn't sound Native American."

She gave Micah the bottle, the baby instantly quieting in her arms. "No, it's not. My father wasn't from the reservation the way my mother was. Her last name was Blackhawk. Ava Blackhawk."

"Are your parents still alive?"

"No." She grimaced, then added, "My parents were killed in a motorcycle accident."

"I'm sorry to hear that." He felt bad for dragging out

painful memories. As his gaze rested on Micah, a stunning realization hit hard.

Rebecca's son was likely the heir to the Woodward fortune.

Garrett's gut clenched in horror. What in the world had he gotten himself into? Was this the motive behind Rebecca's murder? Had she been shot to prevent her from inheriting her father's billion-dollar estate?

As much as he hated the idea, it made sense. Who stood to inherit if Rebecca and Micah were gone?

He had no idea, but he assumed it could be any of Rebecca's aunts, uncles or cousins. She was an only child, but there were likely other Woodward family members out there, just itching to get their hands on Robert Woodward's money.

Thinking about the family members helped steady his nerves. He didn't want anything to do with that much money. He sensed that would only bring trouble.

But he wasn't about to give Micah over to some of those same family members, either.

What a mess. He turned from Liz and the baby, and hurried back to the computer. A quick search on Robert and Rebecca Woodward brought up another article, with a picture. Robert had his arm around his daughter, claiming her to be the next CEO and owner of the company. The words on the screen only cemented what he'd already feared.

Whoever stood to inherit it if Rebecca and Micah were gone was now the top suspect in Rebecca's murder.

He began digging into Robert Woodward's extended family. He needed a starting place before he approached Liam with a list of suspects.

"Garrett?" Liz's soft voice interrupted his thoughts. "I'm going to rest in one of the guest rooms. I'll keep Micah next to me in his car seat."

"Thank you." He felt guilty for taking advantage of her kindness. "Either room is fine."

"Thanks." She glanced down at her bloody scrubs. "I may need to borrow a T-shirt to wear."

"Of course." He jumped up from his seat, taking a moment to rummage through his things. He found a pair of athletic shorts with a drawstring and a navy blue T-shirt. Liz took the items gratefully and disappeared into the bathroom to change.

Micah was asleep again in his carrier just inside the bedroom door. It occurred to him that the baby slept a lot. Maybe that was the case with all newborns—what did he know?

Nothing, and wasn't that the understatement of the year.

He turned to head back to his desk. He'd already found mention of Robert's younger brother, Edward, and his two kids, Elaine and Jeremy.

The two kids weren't married, from what he could tell, but they all stood to inherit now that Rebecca was gone.

Unless, of course, everything had been left to Micah.

His stomach knotted at the thought as he continued his search. His eyes began to blur from exhaustion, so he finally shut the computer down. Stretching his muscles, he turned off the kitchen light, plunging the house in darkness. When his eyes adjusted, he performed a quick check, going from window to window to look outside.

Did anyone in the Woodward family know that he was Micah's biological father? Was that part of the reason the baby was in danger?

A flash of movement from the shed in his backyard caught his eye. Garrett froze, keeping to the side of the window and hopefully out of sight.

Was someone out there? Or had it been one of the many white-tailed deer that roamed the woods around his property?

Moving with extreme caution, he slipped his service weapon from the holster and held the gun down at his side. Everything outside remained still for several long minutes.

His imagination? Maybe. Still, he continued to wait and watch.

There! The shadow moved again, going from one tree to the next.

Not a deer, but a man.

Garrett didn't dare use his phone, for fear the light from the screen would call attention to him. He waited until he saw the shadow move again, coming another few feet closer to the house.

This time, he saw the gun.

Easing back from the window, he moved quickly into the guest room, where Liz lay on the bed. "Liz? We need to get out of here."

"What?" She lifted her head, looking at him sleepily. "Why?"

"The gunman is outside." He needed backup; he would have gone after the guy himself if not for the need to keep Liz and Micah safe.

He grabbed the baby's carrier and hurried back into the kitchen. After stuffing the few baby supplies Liz had removed back into the diaper bag, he headed to the door. "You and Micah are going to slide into the back seat. You'll have to hold him until we're safe, understand?"

Liz's eyes were wide with fright as she nodded.

He eased open the door, hoping and praying there wasn't another gunman waiting by his vehicle. He didn't see one, so he didn't hesitate. "Now," he whispered.

Liz sprinted toward the car, with Garrett hot on her heels.

He thrust the baby carrier and diaper bag into the back seat, then quickly climbed behind the wheel.

The minute he started the engine, he saw movement. The gunman was running toward them.

He thrust the gearshift in Reverse and hit the gas, sending the SUV barreling backward down the driveway as the sound of gunfire rang out for the second time that evening.

THREE

*P*lease, Lord, keep us safe!

Liz held on to the baby carrier, fumbling with the seat belt as Garrett shot down the driveway. The sound of gunfire made her place her body between Micah's carrier and the back seat so she could shield him from any stray bullets.

The gunfire stopped, but she didn't move from her position.

Garrett hit the brake, shifted gears and then punched the gas. They jolted forward, speeding away from his log cabin. She couldn't see the road, but that was okay; her job was to keep Micah safe.

The baby cried, no doubt from the sound of gunfire. She placed the pacifier in his mouth, crooning to him.

"It's okay, Micah. You're safe. We love you. God loves you."

"Are either of you hurt?" Garrett asked in a clipped tone.

"No." She decided being scared to death didn't count as *hurt.* "I'd like to get Micah's carrier secured, though."

There was a long pause as Garrett turned the SUV in a different direction. Then he pulled over to the side of the road. "Make it quick."

She almost snapped at him, then took a deep breath and went to work. After a minute, she was able to get the seat belt secured, holding the carrier in place. Then she buckled her own seat belt. "Okay, we're ready."

Garrett's response was to pull away from the side of the road and to hit the gas again, reaching highway speeds in a span of five seconds. She understood his concern to stay well ahead of the gunman, but she found herself holding on to the door handle, anyway.

"How did they find us?" The wooded green scenery passed by in a blur.

"I don't know." He spoke through clenched teeth. "I made sure we weren't followed from headquarters to my place. It doesn't make sense that the gunman could know my name, much less my address."

She shivered despite the warm summer temps. He was right about one thing: nothing about this scenario made sense. Glancing at Micah, she was glad to see he'd fallen back to sleep, the pacifier lying in the carrier next to the stuffed bunny she'd bought for Willow. The one she'd almost buried with her daughter.

That thought brought her back to the present. Who would want to hurt a baby? How could this little boy be a threat to anyone?

"Where are we going?" Liz tried not to sound as exhausted as she felt. Running from gunfire was wreaking havoc on her equilibrium.

"We'll have to find a motel." Garrett sounded less tense now that they were safe. "But I'd like to see Rebecca's car. There may be something to learn from the vehicle."

"What if a gunman is there?" As much as she liked the idea of being close to her clinic, a wave of apprehension hit hard.

"We left him at my place, remember? Which reminds me." He used his hands-free function to make a call. "Gloria? It's Garrett. Someone fired shots at my house. I need the area searched for the shooter, then combed for evidence."

"I'll send Wyatt, ASAP."

"Send Abby with him. I don't want them to walk into an ambush. And let them know it's likely the same shooter that was outside our headquarters two hours ago. If possible, I'd like the shell casings tested to see if they're a match."

"Roger that. Take care, Garrett." The woman's voice sounded brisk and businesslike, but the way she used his first name gave Liz the impression they didn't stand on formality here.

"Will do." Garrett disconnected from the call, then met her gaze in the rearview mirror. "Are there motels near your clinic?"

"There's one in Liberty, but it only has ten rooms and is nothing fancy. There are nicer ones closer to Green Bay."

"I don't need fancy. I can drop you and the baby at the motel before I head over to check the vehicle."

"I need to leave a new note for my patients on my clinic door, anyway, to let them know I'll be away for longer than planned." She frowned, then added, "Honestly, Garrett? I'd feel better if we stayed together."

"Then that's what we'll do." His easy acceptance of the plan helped her relax. He met her gaze in the rearview mirror again. "Try to get some sleep."

Sleep? He had to be kidding. On the heels of that thought, she yawned, finding the rhythmic sound of wheels on the road soothing. Micah must have liked it, too, as he continued to sleep.

Staring down at his adorable face, she thought of her daughter, Willow. Giving birth to a stillborn baby had been the most traumatic experience of her life. Her husband had blamed her for the loss because she'd been working long hours and hadn't noticed right away that the baby had stopped moving. And for years, she'd blamed herself, too. When her husband, Eric, had been diagnosed with a rare form of leukemia, he refused medical treatment. Less than a year later, he was gone.

Liz grieved Willow's loss more than Eric's, which seemed wrong. Yet her relationship with Eric had grown so contentious, she'd been relieved when he left her to move in with another woman on the reservation.

In the three years since losing her family, Liz had found God and accepted Jesus as her savior. With that, she'd dedicated her life to helping other Native American women and other low-income mothers avoid the same devastation. Even those who didn't much like Western medicine.

But deep down, she'd often wondered why other babies were allowed to live, while Willow hadn't.

Liz must have dozed, because she jerked awake when the vehicle suddenly slowed. Blinking in the darkness, her gaze landed on the Cadillac sitting along the side of the road.

"That's the car I saw on my way to Green Lake." She craned her neck to see better. "I remember thinking that had to be Rebecca's car since no one out here drives anything that expensive."

"You're probably right." Garrett frowned. "I wonder if the caddy is new. She wasn't driving that when I saw her ten months ago."

"I could be wrong," she admitted. "It just looked out of place here."

"I believe it's hers." Garrett drove past the seemingly abandoned vehicle, his gaze raking the area. She couldn't help peering out her window, too, searching for any sign of danger.

After a short ride, he turned around to head back to the

car. Then he made another turn so that he could park behind the caddy. She noticed the car was pointed in the direction of her clinic and wondered if this was where Rebecca had been shot.

Just thinking of her being shot and making it two miles to her clinic gave her a new appreciation for the woman's sheer grit and determination. Looking at Micah, she understood Rebecca had done what was necessary to save her unborn child.

"Liz?"

She glanced up. "Yes?"

"I'd like you to get behind the wheel, just in case something goes awry."

"Okay." She pushed open her door, glancing at Micah. She was glad the baby was still sleeping, but she knew his peaceful slumber wouldn't last long. After closing the door as silently as possible, she slid in behind the wheel.

Flashlight in hand, Garrett stealthily approached the caddy. He took his time inspecting the outer portion of the vehicle before shining the light through the windows.

Liz gripped the steering wheel tightly and alternated between watching Garrett and scanning the wooded area around them.

She felt certain Garrett was right about how the gunman was likely in Green Lake rather than beating them out here in the middle of nowhere, just inside the rez.

But that didn't ease her apprehension.

After what seemed like eons—but was likely only ten minutes—Garrett opened the caddy's door. A minute later, he closed it again, then turned to head back to the SUV.

She pushed out from the vehicle so he could get in behind the wheel, then frowned when she saw he had a slip of paper in his hand. "What is it? What did you find?"

He looked at her for a long moment, then showed it to her. She gasped when she saw her name, cell number and clinic address on the slip of paper.

"Me?" she whispered. "Rebecca specifically came all this way to see me? Why?"

Garrett's intense gaze drilled into hers. "I was hoping you could tell me."

She shook her head, leaning weakly against the SUV. It didn't make sense. Sure, her services to low-income mothers were well-known among people living in the area, especially within the reservation. She also worked closely with an OB in Green Bay for cases outside her area of expertise.

But outside of this area, she doubted anyone knew her. There was no rational explanation why a woman like Rebecca, who had money and access to top-notch OB specialists, had come all this way to see her.

Or why she'd been followed and shot to death along the way.

Garrett watched Liz's reaction closely, believing she'd been thrown completely off-balance by seeing her name and contact information on the slip of paper he'd noticed halfway under the passenger seat of the caddy.

"I don't understand," she whispered.

Yeah, that was putting it mildly. He pocketed the slip of paper, then reached over to open her door. "Let's head over to your clinic."

She didn't move. "Did you find anything else in the car?"

"I didn't find what I'd expected." He gestured for her to get in. "We'll talk along the way."

Moving slowly, she slid in beside Micah's car seat. He closed the door, then climbed in behind the wheel. Shifting the car into gear, he pulled out onto the highway.

Micah began to squirm and cry. Liz did her best to soothe him. "My clinic isn't far. Take the second road to the right."

"Okay." He watched her bend over the baby. "Are you going to wait until then to feed him?"

"Yes." She met his gaze in the rearview mirror. "What did you find, Garrett?"

"What I didn't find was blood or a bullet hole inside the vehicle. I assumed she'd been shot while sitting behind the wheel. Did you notice the flat tire?" When she nodded, he said, "Makes me wonder if the bad guys shot out the tire, then gave chase. But you said she was shot in the chest, so that part doesn't make sense."

"Yes, that's correct—she was shot on the upper-left side of her chest." She frowned. "There was no exit wound, either."

He considered that for a moment. "Rebecca must have been far away when she was hit, then. A gunshot from close range would have likely gone all the way through."

Liz closed her eyes for a moment. "That's horrible. It's all so awful."

"Tell me about it," he muttered, half under his breath. The entire situation was difficult to comprehend. Rebecca hadn't gotten lost on her way to find him in Green Lake, like he'd assumed. No, Liz's clinic had been her destination all along. She'd come way out here to seek Liz's help in delivering her baby.

Their baby. Micah.

Why? Rebecca had money and access to exceptional obstetric care in Chicago. Why come all this way? And who had killed her? He felt certain the gunman had shot Rebecca to kill her and the baby.

If not for Liz's skill, he would have succeeded.

He was still getting accustomed to the idea of having a

son, but the idea that someone intended to kill the infant made his blood boil. He made a silent promise to never let that happen.

Taking the second right-hand turn as Liz had directed, he saw the clinic up ahead, roughly fifty yards away. He frowned, not liking how the building was rather isolated. He didn't see any other houses or businesses nearby.

Did Liz work there alone? Or did she have help?

Scanning the area for threats, he pulled up next to the building. Then he took a moment to turn the vehicle around so they could get away quickly if needed.

Micah's wails grew louder now, so he shut down the car and jumped out. He opened Liz's door. "What can I do?"

"Take him for me. I'll make a bottle." She released the seat belt and handed the baby carrier to him. He tried to soothe the baby as Liz opened the clinic door and stepped inside.

The clinic was spacious, with a room full of supplies off to one side. The exam room was in complete disarray; there were towels tossed all over the floor, covering puddles of blood.

Rebecca's blood. Her body was gone, but the scene of destruction had remained. He swallowed hard, grieving for the loss of his friend.

What happened, Rebecca? Why didn't you call me?

There was nothing but silence for an answer.

Liz stared at the mess for a moment, then led the way through another door, where a very small and cramped living area was located.

Shaking himself out of his sorrow, he followed Liz, not surprised to see she'd sacrificed her living area in favor of making sure the clinic was functional. As she moved around the small kitchen, he unbuckled Micah from the carrier and gently cradled the crying baby in his arms.

As before, he was struck by how tiny he was. His small face was beet red and scrunched up in anger over being so hungry.

"Hang on, little man. Food is on the way."

"Have a seat on the sofa." Liz was shaking the bottle to dissolve the formula. "I'd like you to feed him."

"Me?" He sat but stared up at her with wide eyes. "I don't know how."

"Time to learn, don't you think?" She adjusted the baby in his arms, then handed him the bottle. "He's your son. Practice makes perfect."

Thankfully, Micah took the bottle without difficulty. He found it hard to tear his gaze away from his son's peaceful expression—so different from the wailing just seconds earlier.

A wave of responsibility hit hard. This little baby was completely helpless, dependent on Garrett and Liz, at least for now, to provide for him.

He wanted to assure the little boy he wouldn't fail in his role as his protector, but considering how close the gunman had gotten to them—twice in as many hours—the words caught in his throat.

As soon as Liz finished up here and Micah had eaten his fill, they'd head to a motel for what was left of the night. And after that?

He sighed heavily. Other than checking in with Wyatt and Abby, he had no clue.

Liz used her computer to presumably send an email to her patients and print out a new note to attach to her door. When those tasks were finished, she packed more items in the diaper bag and took a moment to change into fresh clothes: a soft forest green short-sleeved shirt and worn blue jeans.

"Micah fell asleep," he whispered, setting the bottle aside.

"Put him up on your shoulder and rub his back in sooth-ing circles. He may need to burp."

"Ah, okay." He carefully moved the baby to his shoul-der, half-afraid he'd drop him. "We should hit the road."

"We will, as soon as I change him." She flashed a smile. "Or rather, *you* change him. It's all part of learning how to take care of your son."

"I'm sure it's not that hard to change a diaper." Messy, but not difficult.

He'd underestimated just how messy and difficult, but he managed to get the job done. Liz took the baby as he washed up at the sink.

Through the window, a flash of light in the distance caught his attention. He stared at the area for a long mo-ment, and when the light didn't reappear, he turned away, relieved to see Liz had buckled Micah in the carrier.

"How close is the next property?" He shouldered the di-aper bag and reached for the car seat handle. "I saw a light outside, north of here."

Her dark eyes widened. "There's nothing close by. This was an abandoned property before I moved in. The build-ing came with five acres of land."

That's what he was afraid of. "We need to go." He shut off the kitchen light, plunging the room into darkness. "Fol-low me."

Envisioning the clinic layout in his mind, Garrett care-fully made his way through the building and toward the door, holding Micah's carrier at a level high enough to avoid the exam table.

Was he overreacting to the flash of light? He didn't think so. Maybe it was nothing more than a car coming down the highway, disappearing behind trees. Yet he couldn't ignore his instincts screaming at him to get Micah and Liz out of there.

Pausing at the door, he opened it a crack, listening intently. After a full minute of silence, he stepped outside, moving softly toward the vehicle.

Liz kept close, taking just a moment to lock the door behind them before crossing to the car. He hesitated, knowing that the SUV dome light would come on the moment he opened the car door.

It was a situation that couldn't be helped, although he wished he'd had the forethought to take the bulb out before going inside. Then again, he'd thought coming here would be safe since they'd left the gunman at his place.

Was anywhere safe?

"We need to move quickly," he said in a low voice. "Ready?"

She nodded.

He opened the door to the back seat. Liz slid in and reached for Micah's carrier. He handed it over, dropped the diaper bag on the floor and then closed the door. While she buckled Micah in, he opened the driver's-side door.

A twig snapped. Someone was in the woods!

He slid into the seat and started the SUV, thankful he'd parked it for a quick getaway. He hit the gas, moving down the driveway to the road.

In the rearview mirror, he saw a dark shadow burst from the woods. Another gunman!

He pushed his foot down on the gas pedal as the man behind them fired several rounds from his weapon. Garrett wanted to know how in the world this guy had found them. When he heard the ping of bullet against metal, he knew they'd been hit.

"Garrett?" Liz's voice trembled with fear.

"Hang on." He continued driving, silently praying the gunman's bullet hadn't damaged anything major. They made it all the way to the road before he glanced at the gas gauge. The needle dropped right before his eyes.

He didn't let up on the accelerator, praying they'd have enough fuel to get far enough away from the gunman.

But as the needle continued to fall and the engine slowed, he knew that wasn't going to happen. He wrenched the wheel, pulling off to the side of the road seconds before the engine died completely.

They would have to escape the gunman on foot.

FOUR

"Why are we stopping?" Liz tried to keep calm, but her voice trembled with fear. She couldn't believe the gunman had found them at her clinic!

Was he the same one who had been in Green Lake? Or a different one? Were there several gunmen after them? And if so, why were they all seemingly intent on killing an innocent baby?

"Gas tank has been hit." Garrett pushed open his door. "Get Micah's carrier unbuckled, then grab the diaper bag. Hurry."

She quickly did as he asked, praying for strength. Garrett opened the back passenger door and lifted Micah's carrier from the seat. Looping the strap of the diaper bag over her shoulder, she scrambled out of the vehicle to join him.

"Follow me." He didn't hesitate to break into a loping jog, heading toward a dense section of the woods. She managed to keep up but wasn't sure how long she'd be able to run so fast as Garrett's long legs ate up the yards. Good thing she'd changed into darker clothing.

Thankfully, he slowed his pace once they reached the shelter of the trees. But not by much. He moved swiftly, his head swiveling back and forth as he scanned their surroundings.

She had no doubt he expected the gunmen to show up at any moment. The mere idea of being stalked by these men made her shiver.

Liz did her best not to gasp for breath as she moved through the trees. Her Native American ancestors would know how to melt into the forest, but as much as she liked the rural surroundings of her clinic, she was no expert at hiding in the woods. Through the darkness, she could barely see the dark shape of Garrett's body up ahead.

Guide us to safety, Lord!

As if reading her mind, Garrett glanced over his shoulder. Slowing his pace, he waited for her to catch up. The diaper bag was navy blue, with a pattern of white giraffes on the outside, and she feared it would be a beacon to anyone searching for them.

Garrett didn't say anything but held her gaze for a moment as if asking if she was okay. She nodded, deciding not to voice her fears. Especially related to Micah. The baby was sleeping for now, but what would happen when he awoke? Newborns cried and that, too, would lead the bad guys to them.

Her foot got tangled in a fallen tree branch. She sucked in a breath and held on to the tree trunk for support. Garrett continued moving, so she forced herself to do the same, understanding the importance of remaining silent and hidden.

Yet how long could they survive in the woods? Mentally reviewing the contents of the diaper bag, she remembered placing two cans of premade formula inside, along with the container of powdered mix. The cans would buy them a little time before they'd need water to make another bottle.

Her own stomach growled with hunger; she hadn't eaten much for dinner. Ignoring the sensation, she hoped the rumbles wouldn't be loud enough to draw unwanted attention.

After what seemed like an hour but was likely much less, Garrett stopped at the base of a large oak. He set Micah's carrier down, then gestured for her to sit, too.

"Rest." His low whisper tickled her ear.

She nodded and dropped to the ground beside the baby. While it felt good to rest her muscles, her body remained tense with fear. How long before the gunmen found them?

Imagining the worst wasn't helpful. Garrett was armed and would protect them, especially Micah. Thinking of the baby had her opening the diaper bag. She felt around inside until she found the can of formula.

Reassured, she held it up for Garrett to see. Thankfully, the can had a pop top, so she could easily open it.

"Do you need to feed him?" His voice was barely a whisper.

"Not yet," she said. "Hopefully, he'll sleep for a while."

"We need to keep moving."

She grimaced, tucking the can of formula into the bag. She rose, looping the strap over her shoulder. Garrett stood and lifted the baby carrier. Watching as the muscles in his arms bunched, she was grateful for his strength. She doubted she'd have been able to carry the baby carrier this far on her own.

Garrett stealthily moved through the woods. She understood silence was more important than speed, so she placed her feet in the same places he did. She might not be as quiet as he was, but the occasional snap of a twig could be attributed to wildlife moving through the area.

After another twenty minutes, Garrett stopped. She craned her neck to see what he'd found. A large tree branch was hanging down all the way to the ground, creating a small, sheltered area.

After placing Micah's carrier on the ground, he turned

to her. "You should stay here with Micah. I'd like to walk the area to see if I can pick up any sign of the gunman."

Swallowing hard, she nodded. "Okay."

"Will you be okay for a short while?" He searched her gaze.

"Of course." She forced a reassuring smile. What choice did she have? She trusted Garrett's instincts in deeming it important to scout the area. His expertise, not hers.

His smile shot her pulse into high gear. It was the wrong time to be aware of how handsome he was. Grateful for the darkness that hid her flushed cheeks, she lowered herself down on the ground, using the tree branches around her as shelter. Garrett lightly touched her shoulder before moving away.

She shivered, but not from the cold. What was wrong with her? Where had this weird attraction to Garrett come from? She hadn't been the least bit interested in anything remotely resembling a relationship since her husband, Eric, had left her for another woman—one, he'd claimed, who was more kind and caring than she was.

She let out a soundless sigh. No sense in reminiscing about the past. Especially since she knew Garrett only wanted her to help with caring for the baby. She couldn't turn her back on this father and newborn son.

Her feelings were irrelevant. The most important task looming before her was to keep Micah safe. And she would.

No matter what.

Feeling calmer, she listened intently to the sounds of the night. She was impressed at how quietly Garrett was able to move through the brush. Maybe it was his cop training, or he was an experienced hunter. Either way, she couldn't hear him at all.

The hum of insects, chirping crickets and belching tree

frogs were oddly reassuring. Resting her hand on the sleeping baby, she relaxed against the branches behind her.

For the moment, they were safe. And she couldn't ask for more than that.

Garrett eased through the brush, every one of his senses on full alert. He didn't hear or see anything unusual but wasn't ready to let down his guard.

It was his fault they were in this mess. He shouldn't have come to investigate Rebecca's caddy without backup.

And worse, he'd brought Liz and Micah directly into the line of fire.

The fact that there were so many gunmen made him think they were hired killers. Nothing else made sense. No way had a single gunman take shots at them back at his place only to show up again here at Liz's clinic. How many of them were out there? He had no idea. But he suspected they'd been hired by someone in the Woodward family.

A man or woman determined to eliminate Micah as the heir to the family fortune.

The task of keeping his son and Liz safe loomed before him. When he'd completed a twenty-yard circle around the spot where he'd left them, he returned to the downed tree branch. When he stepped out from behind a tree trunk, Liz startled badly, placing her hand over her heart.

"Sorry," he murmured. "Didn't mean to scare you."

Liz nodded, then lifted a brow in a silent question.

"It's clear." He glanced at the sleeping baby. They couldn't hide out in the woods forever, so he needed to come up with a plan to get them out of here, safely. He dropped down beside her so they could speak quietly. "How much longer do you think he'll sleep?"

She grimaced. "You fed him at the clinic, so he should

be fine for a while yet—although newborns can be unpredictable."

Since he had no personal experience with babies, predictable or not, he shrugged. "I'd like to wait here for a bit before we head back."

Her eyes widened. "Back where?"

"To the caddy." He held her gaze. "I can put the spare on to get us out of here."

"Are you sure that's a good idea?" She looked far from convinced. "Wouldn't the gunmen consider that as our only option, too?"

"It's possible." He gazed around their wooded sanctuary. "But what else can we do? If I call my deputies to pick us up, they'll draw attention, too." He couldn't knowingly put his deputies in danger. "It's better if we sneak up to the caddy on our own."

"I don't know." A frown puckered her brow, and she gnawed on her lower lip. "That seems risky. But I'll go along with whatever you think is best."

Her faith in his abilities only added to the weight of responsibility he carried. He forced himself to sit for a moment, thinking through their options. He could call Wyatt and Abby, but he feared the headlights of their vehicle would be act as a beacon for the gunmen. And he wasn't sure exactly where he and Liz were—just outside Liberty, but he couldn't remember the last mile marker they'd passed.

Maybe a combination of both ideas would work. He leaned toward Liz. "Can you tell me where the closest gas station or grocery store is in relation to your clinic?"

She thought for a moment. "I generally use the gas station we passed on the way. It's probably seven miles or so from the clinic."

He searched his memory. "The Gas and Go station?"

"Yes." She grimaced. "There's really nothing very close to me. Unless you want to head further into the Oneida reservation."

Bringing danger into the reservation didn't seem wise— not to mention, the local cops didn't have jurisdiction there. He shook his head. "No, we'll use the Gas and Go station. But we can't walk seven miles through the woods to get there. I'll stash you and Micah someplace nearby while I work on changing the tire."

"Okay." Her eyes were dark with apprehension. He understood her fear. It seemed the gunmen had been following their every move.

Was it possible that Rebecca had told someone Micah was his child? He wished he understood why she hadn't told him that he was to be a father.

"We'll stay here for a while." He tried to smile reassuringly. "Just pray Micah doesn't wake up crying."

"Maybe we should fill a bottle with premade formula, just in case."

"Good idea."

She rummaged around in the diaper bag and pulled out a can, setting it aside. Then she opened a small bottle, placing a plastic liner inside. When that was ready, she popped the top of the can and poured the contents into the bottle.

It occurred to him that without her generosity, they'd be sitting here with nothing for the baby.

She looked up at him. "The can is supposed to be refrigerated after opening."

"Fill another bottle. We may end up using it sooner than later, anyway. When we get to the gas station, we can buy a cold pack." He didn't want to leave anything behind that the gunmen could find.

"Okay."

While she did as he'd asked, he glanced at his watch, trying to estimate how much time it would take them to head back through the woods to where Rebecca's car was located. He knew the caddy was only two miles from Liz's clinic. They hadn't reached it before his SUV had run out of fuel, but the two vehicles were likely closer than he liked.

Pulling out his phone, he swallowed a groan when he saw there was only one bar of service. Being out in the woods often meant no internet access. Rather than risk making a call, he decided to text Wyatt, hoping he and Abby weren't still processing the crime scene. They'd pulled a double shift to help cover in Jason's absence. Since the trip to Liberty took almost an hour, he thought it likely they'd finished gathering evidence from his house by now.

Are you available? I need backup and a car.

For several minutes, there was no response. Then, finally, an answering text bloomed on the screen.

Yes. What's up?

He thought for a moment, then texted back. Gunfire outside Liberty. Bring two cars. Meet at the Gas and Go on highway 45 but no lights or sirens.

This time there was no delay in the response. Got It. We'll be there ASAP.

Even though he knew Wyatt and Abby wouldn't get there for at least fifty to sixty minutes, he felt better having them on the way.

Now all he needed to do was to get the caddy running

enough to drive them seven miles down the highway—
heading in the opposite direction of Liz's clinic, thankfully.

Then again, the gunmen could easily set up somewhere
along the side of the road, assuming they'd go that way. Yet
what other option did he have?

He turned toward Liz. "Do you have friends on the reservation?"

"No." She shook her head. "I have a few patients who
live there, but I wouldn't feel comfortable showing up at
their house in the middle of the night."

"Okay, then we'll stick with the original plan." Using his
phone, he opened the compass app to make sure he was
heading in the right direction. His dad had often taken him
hunting and insisted he learn to read a compass. His dad had
made sure to test his knowledge, too, purposefully leaving
him alone to get back to their truck.

A test he'd passed with flying colors. His dad had claimed
Garrett had an innate sense of direction.

A skill that would serve him well now.

After he'd mentally plotted their course, he pocketed his
phone and gestured toward the diaper bag. "Grab that and
we'll start heading back. Stay close behind me, okay?"

"Okay." She gamely did as he'd asked.

He lifted the carrier, his muscles taut. The baby wasn't
that heavy, but carrying him in such a way as to prevent
the carrier from striking anything was difficult. He was
forced to carry it higher and farther away from his body
than normal.

Pausing, he glanced back. "Oh, and I'll stop the minute
Micah sounds like he's waking up, so get the bottle ready
right away. Better to feed him a little early than let him cry."

Her dark gaze held his. "I understand."

He knew she was just as worried about giving away their

location as he was. He moved forward, easing through the woods while doing his best to keep a sedate pace for her sake. He'd noticed that she was quieter when she was able to step where he had.

Still, he could hear Liz moving behind him. As they walked, Garrett found himself silently praying for God's strength and guidance as he moved through the woods. He still didn't understand why God had taken Jason from them, but he didn't hesitate to throw himself on His mercy now.

Please, Lord Jesus, grant me the strength and wisdom I need to keep my son and Liz safe from harm!

For the first time in months, praying filled him with a sense of peace. As if God might be there for him after all, despite his anger toward Him.

He continued walking, pausing every so often to listen for sounds that indicated they were not alone. But the night air remained quiet, except for the usual sounds of insects and tree frogs.

After they'd gone a hundred yards, he noticed Micah squirming in his sleep. He stopped and dropped to a crouch. Instantly, Liz came up beside him with a bottle in hand.

Without saying a word, she unbuckled the baby and lifted him into her arms. She quickly offered him the bottle. He latched on, thankfully not breaking into a wailing cry.

Garrett carefully scanned the area but didn't see anything suspicious. If he didn't know better, he'd think they were alone out here.

But he suspected the gunmen had set up somewhere close by.

Maybe they should try to walk the seven miles to the gas station. But as soon as the thought formed, he rejected it. They were vulnerable out here. At least the caddy offered some level of physical protection.

Micah must not have been all the way awake, because he fell back asleep within ten minutes. Liz shrugged and gently set the sleeping infant back in the carrier. He strapped him in as she tucked the bottle in the diaper bag.

Once the baby was settled, he continued walking. The sound of rustling leaves made him freeze, until he caught sight of a white-tailed deer moving away from them.

They must have gotten too close to the deer's bed.

After what seemed like eons but was only another twenty minutes, he caught a glimpse of the road through the trees. He went another ten yards, then veered to the right, heading toward a cluster of three skinny pine trees.

Liz followed close on his heels. When he reached the area, he could see several feet of the highway. And, just barely, the glint of the moon shining off the rear bumper.

Lowering to a crouch, he set Micah's carrier on a soft bed of pine needles. Liz's feet made no sound as she came up beside him. He gave her a reassuring smile. "I'll need you to wait here with Micah, okay?"

She frowned. "We're pretty far from the road. I can barely see it."

"It's only about another ten yards away. Move this way. Can you see the caddy now?"

She nodded. "Yes."

"Good." After slipping his hand in his pocket, he drew out his phone. "Take this. If anything happens, I want you to disappear farther into the woods with Micah and to call Wyatt and Abby. They're two of my best deputies."

Her eyes widened in alarm. "What about you?"

"I'm armed." He pressed the phone into her hand, then gave her the passcode. "Repeat it back to me."

She recited the month and year of his birth, backward.

He bent to press a quick kiss to Micah's head before rising to his feet. "Stay safe."

"You, too."

He nodded, then moved away, determined to execute this plan without failing. Getting through the woods to the highway wouldn't take long, but he knew that crossing the road meant being exposed to anyone watching nearby.

He stood near a large tree for several long moments, searching the foliage for anything out of place. Then he gazed up at the sky. There were a few clouds drifting toward the half-moon that illuminated the sky. The second the clouds moved over the moon, he darted out from his hiding spot and ran to the abandoned caddy, then ducked behind it.

Earlier, he'd noticed the keys lying on the driver's-side floor, so he'd picked them up. He used them now to open the trunk. As he lifted the spare and the jack out from the well, the clouds finished passing the moon, and the area around him brightened noticeably.

He went to work, using the jack to lift the rear of the sedan. Changing the tire didn't take long, although he felt exposed the entire time. When he finished, he didn't bother to replace the tire and jack in the trunk. Time was of the essence.

Still in a crouch, he rounded the rear of the vehicle to get into the driver's seat. The car was pointed toward the clinic, but he needed to go the other way. When he opened the car door, he heard the barest sound of a footstep behind him.

Whirling around with his weapon in hand, he dropped as gunfire rang out. Pain lanced his arm as he instinctively fired back, praying he wasn't surrounded and would be able to escape.

FIVE

More gunfire! Liz's heart lodged in her throat as she huddled over Micah in his carrier. Through a gap in the trees, she watched as Garrett exchanged gunfire with a man dressed in black. Garrett's bullet struck the guy in the chest, and he fell backward, hitting the pavement with a thud.

She stared at the downed gunman for a long moment, trying to ascertain if he was breathing. But she was too far away to be sure one way or the other.

A bullet to the chest didn't mean he was dead; Rebecca's injury proved that. Though Liz knew that Rebecca had had a reason to live—an important reason to make her way to the clinic.

She'd pushed herself to survive, for the sake of her baby.

Garrett rose and went to the injured gunman to check for a pulse. Then he checked the guy's pockets, pulling out a disposable phone and a bundle of cash. Only when he glanced in her direction did she stand, carrying Micah's carrier as she emerged from her hiding spot.

The nurse in her wanted to provide first aid to the injured man, but the baby's safety had to come first. Garrett opened the back door of the caddy so she could buckle Micah inside.

"He's dead. We need to get out of here."

She glanced over her shoulder to find him standing directly in front of her, scanning the woods for threats. She swallowed hard and whispered, "I know."

Within minutes, they were settled in the caddy, heading to the gas station. She couldn't relax, fearing more gunmen would pop out of the woods and start shooting at them.

After a few moments of silence, she asked, "Did you find an ID on him?"

"No." Garrett gestured to the cheap phone and cash he'd taken from the dead man's pockets, which he'd tucked into the center console. "I'll get my deputies to see if they can lift prints and get some information on the phone itself."

She stared at him through the darkness. "Don't you think it's strange he didn't have an ID on him?"

"Professionals don't carry IDs." Garrett's voice was grim. "He is obviously a hired hit man."

"Who would hire someone to kill a baby?" Liz had trouble comprehending what was happening to them. "What threat does Micah pose?"

Garrett arched his brow. "He's likely the heir to the Woodward fortune. With Rebecca and Micah out of the picture, Rebecca's cousins are set to inherit a billion dollars when her father dies. And it just so happens Robert was recently diagnosed with stage four pancreatic cancer."

A cold chill snaked down her spine. This was all about money. Killing an innocent baby to get their grubby hands on a fortune. "That's evil."

"Yes, it is." Garrett's gaze went from the rearview mirror to the highway ahead of them. He wasn't driving fast; the caddy lurched to one side, the spare tire smaller than the others. "The gas station is up ahead. We'll have to wait for my deputies, Wyatt and Abby, to get here. They're bringing a car for us to use but then will need to head back to where I left the dead gunman."

"I hope you don't get in trouble for shooting him." She hated to think Garrett's career would suffer because of this. "I couldn't see everything clearly, but I heard multiple gunshots. I know you only fired in self-defense."

"Yeah. And I have the injury to prove it."

Injury? She gasped. "What happened? Where are you hit?"

"I'm fine. The bullet grazed my arm." He downplayed the wound, and she had to assume the injury was to his left arm because his right side looked fine. "We can get some stuff at the gas station to patch it up."

"I have gauze in the diaper bag, too." She wished she'd brought more supplies from her clinic. Unfortunately, there was no going back now.

In fact, she wasn't sure they'd be safe anywhere.

Lights from the gas station brightened the otherwise dark sky. Normally, she'd be thrilled to be near other people.

But instead, a cloud of apprehension hung over her. Bright lights meant being a clear target for the gunmen.

She put a hand on his arm. "Maybe we shouldn't go to the gas station yet. What if the gunmen are there?"

"I understand your concern. My plan is to drive past it and find a place to hide the caddy. You and Micah will wait for me to clear the place."

She shivered but didn't argue. So far, Garrett had succeeded in protecting them. She only wished he could be safe, too.

There were no cars parked in front of the fuel pumps as they drove past. The sign outside the building indicated the gas station was open twenty-four seven.

Soon, the lights were behind them as Garrett kept driving. He abruptly slowed the vehicle, then came to a stop. She glanced around curiously. "Why here?"

"Hang on." He put the car in Reverse and turned the wheel to back into a wooded area. Craning her neck, she realized he intended to hide the caddy between two large pine trees. He shut down the engine, then angled toward her. "You and Micah should be safe here. It won't take me long to head back to make sure the gas station is clear."

"I didn't see any cars there."

"I know. But the way things have been going, I want to be certain. Here are the keys." He tucked them into her hand, then wrapped his fingers around hers. "Give me your cell number, I'll call when it's okay for you to drive back to the gas station, okay?"

"That works." She gave him the number, watching as he entered it in his phone.

"Ready?" He glanced up at her.

She forced a smile, wishing she didn't have to let him go. He held her gaze for a long second before releasing her and pushing out of the car. She eased up over the center console to drop into the driver's seat, which held the warmth of his body.

As before, Garrett moved quietly through the trees, melting into the forest. She was the one with Native American blood in her veins, but he was much better at moving swiftly and quietly. She twisted around to see over the edge of Micah's carrier. Thankfully, the newborn slept peacefully.

She bent her head, closing her eyes for a moment to pray: *Lord Jesus, keep this innocent baby safe in Your loving arms. Amen.*

God had brought Rebecca to her clinic and had sent her to Garrett with the baby. If she hadn't have escaped, Liz knew she and Micah would both be dead.

Shaking off the horrible thought, she took heart in knowing that Garrett's deputies would be there soon. He'd mentioned they were bringing another vehicle for them to use, too. Hopefully, one the gunmen wouldn't recognize.

As the minutes ticked by slowly, her apprehension grew. What if Garrett had been caught and killed? She told herself not to imagine the worst, but it wasn't easy to let go of the fear that plagued her.

She frowned when she noticed the sky was lighter near the road. It took a second for her to realize the faint illumination she saw through the pine branches was from a car. Garrett had tucked her so far back, she couldn't see the vehicle until it passed directly across the highway in front of her.

Her heart thudded painfully against her ribs. Who was behind the wheel? Another gunman? The deputies? Someone else?

Seconds after the vehicle passed her line of sight, a second vehicle drove by. Two cars. She relaxed her deathlike grip on the key fob. The vehicles must belong to Garrett's deputies.

Yet her phone didn't ring.

Please, Lord, keep us all safe in Your care!

Garrett had taken his time scouting around the gas station, unwilling to make another mistake. The last gunman had gotten far too close. He inched his way through the woods, making a circle around the gas station. Once he'd cleared the building, he'd call Liz to let her know it was safe to drive over. Suddenly, he noticed lights approaching in the distance.

Out here, in the middle of nowhere, it was easy to see oncoming traffic. Glancing at his watch, he realized that if the car belonged to Wyatt and Abby, they'd made good time.

Then again, anyone could be driving along the highway, even at two in the morning. Could be another gunman, but he doubted it.

If the hired killer was behind the wheel, he wouldn't drive up with his headlights on. He'd be hiding in the woods, the way the gunman had back at the clinic.

Still, he remained hidden until he noticed the vehicle slow and pull into the gas station. On the heels of that SUV, another pulled in behind him.

Wyatt and Abby to the rescue.

Garrett emerged from the trees, crossing over to meet his deputies. Wyatt's gaze was somber as Garrett approached. "You're bleeding."

"It's fine. Thanks for coming."

"Where's the woman and the baby?" Abby asked, joining them. She held out a set of keys for him. "Are they okay?"

"They are. I stashed them a little over a half mile from here." He sighed, then added, "I shot a man about seven miles back. He's the one who creased my arm. I took his disposable cell and cash from his pocket. They're in the caddy where Liz and Micah are hiding out. I need you to call the homicide in to whatever jurisdiction we're in. It didn't happen on the reservation. We're in Brown County. Their sheriff's department needs to know. Also, we need to get information on the dead guy's identity."

Wyatt let out a low whistle. "You've been busy."

"Yeah, well, Micah is in danger from members of his own family." Garrett still had trouble believing the infant was his son. "The short story is that Rebecca's father is dying, and our son is the heir to the Woodward fortune."

"You're joking." Abby looked shocked. He wasn't sure if it was from the news that he had a son or that the baby would inherit a fortune. Probably both.

"I'm not. And the numerous gunmen that have staked out various locations where Rebecca may have taken the boy is proof." Garrett pulled his phone from his pocket. "I'll call Liz, tell her it's okay to drive back here."

After he made the call, Wyatt asked, "Whoever hired these gunmen knows you're the baby's father."

He nodded slowly. "Yeah. Which is difficult to comprehend since I didn't know until Liz showed up with the baby on my doorstep."

"Rebecca must have confided in someone," Abby mused. "A best friend, maybe?"

He'd have thought *he* was her best friend. Then again, they'd gone beyond friendship, hadn't they? He winced at the memory. "I knew Rebecca from the summers she spent in Green Lake. Her father had a place there but sold it a few years ago. It's on one of those vacation-rental apps. Rebecca rented it last September, and that's when we reconnected."

He stared at the road, waiting for Liz and Micah. When he saw a vehicle come out onto the highway and head toward them, he turned back to his deputies. "I need your help. As soon as you learn anything about the gunman back there, please call me. I can only do so much investigating while keeping Liz and Micah safe."

"That reminds me, we brought you a computer, too." Abby gestured toward the SUV she'd driven. "It's in the front seat."

He nodded in admiration. "What made you think of that?"

She exchanged a knowing look with Wyatt, and the two shared a wry smile. "We know what it's like to be on the run from bad guys, like when the Mafia was after me and my father. Oh, and I tucked spare cash in the laptop bag." Her expression turned serious. "I think it's best for you and Liz to stay off-grid."

"Thank you." He was impressed with the extent of their support. Liz pulled up next to the SUV. First, he removed the cell phone and cash, handing it to Wyatt. Then he unhooked Micah from the back seat. He reached for the diaper bag, too, but Liz took it from his fingers.

"We need to go inside and get medical supplies for your arm," she said.

"Okay. Liz, these two deputies are Wyatt and Abby Kane." He made quick introductions. "Liz Templeton is a midwife. She delivered Micah before Rebecca died of a bullet wound to the chest."

"It's nice to meet you." Abby took Liz's hand, giving her a warm smile. "Wyatt and I have been praying for your safety—and Garrett's, too."

"Don't forget Micah," Liz said.

"We won't," Wyatt assured her. "But you'd better hurry. Grab your supplies and get as far away from here as possible."

Garrett had the same niggling feeling that they'd already lingered too long. He crossed over to strap Micah's car seat into the back of the SUV, then turned to give Liz some cash. "Go inside to buy what you need. Grab something to eat, too. I don't know where we'll end up staying."

"Okay." Liz handed him the diaper bag, then hurried inside.

"I wish there was more we could do for you," Wyatt said. "If not for the dead guy, we could escort you somewhere safe."

"We'll be okay." Garrett already felt better knowing they had cash, a computer and a different vehicle. "You've been a huge help already. Stay in touch."

"Will do." Wyatt clapped him on the back, then opened the driver's-side door of his vehicle. Abby surprised Garrett with a quick hug before joining her husband. They drove off, heading to where he'd left the dead gunman lying in the road.

He didn't like knowing he'd killed a man. Even in self-defense. It would have been better if he'd been able to arrest the guy and question him.

Gazing at his son, he understood that he'd done what was necessary to save the baby's life. When Liz came out of the gas station with a large plastic bag, he didn't hesitate to jump up in the driver's seat.

"In addition to the gauze and tape, I bought us each power bars and several bottles of water." She set the bag on the floor at her feet next to the laptop bag, then latched the seat belt. "We should be set for a while."

"Good." He pulled out of the gas station, taking the highway in the opposite direction of where Wyatt and Abby were working on the gunman. "We'll head west on Highway 28."

"Okay." She unwrapped a power bar and handed it to him, then opened a bottle of water and set it in the cupholder at his elbow. "I'll need to take care of your arm soon."

"Once we find a safe place to stay." It wouldn't be soon, but that didn't matter. He wanted to get as far away from both Green Lake and Brown County as possible.

The power bar was just what he needed, and he washed it down with a healthy slug of water. The nourishment helped keep him focused despite his fatigue. He needed to stay alert for any sign of danger.

If he were honest, he would admit to feeling as if they should head straight across the border to Minnesota. Yet they couldn't keep running like this forever. Micah wouldn't be safe until they uncovered the real culprit.

At the next intersection, he turned right and continued along the winding highway. When he saw a sign that indicated the small town of Viroqua was about twenty miles away, he decided that would be a good destination.

If he remembered correctly, there were some Amish

farms along the north side of Viroqua. And the town itself was quaint, but there was a decent-sized medical center there, too. He wasn't hurt badly, but he was a little concerned about his son. At some point, the baby should be seen by a pediatrician. Not that he doubted Liz's medical expertise, but he knew from when Liam and Shauna gave birth to their daughter, Ciara, that the pediatrician had stopped in to examine her while she and Shauna were still in the hospital.

Liz was silent as they drove through the night. Micah slept the entire ride, too. Figured the little guy would sleep soundly now that they weren't hiding in the woods.

Thankfully, there was no traffic on the road, so they made good time. When he saw the welcome sign for Viroqua, he slowed and pulled into the driveway of a lower-budget motel. "Hope you don't mind."

She shrugged as she pushed open the car door. "You've seen where I live. I don't need anything fancy."

"Wait here," he suggested. "It's summer, but I'll try to get us connecting rooms."

She nodded. "Micah will need a bottle and a change soon."

As if on cue, the little boy began to cry. Garrett hurried inside, knowing Liz would take care of his son. Then he abruptly stopped, realizing that was his job.

It wasn't fair to take advantage of Liz's sweet nature.

Glancing back, he noticed she already had the baby in her arms. He forced himself to head inside to secure their rooms. From now on, he'd do his best to be Micah's caregiver.

Liz wouldn't be with him forever.

The twinge in the region of his heart made no sense, so he ignored it. Luckily, the sleepy clerk had two adjoining rooms, which she allowed him to pay for in cash. Grateful, he took the two keys and went back outside.

Liz sat in the front seat, giving Micah a bottle. But he was fussy, not wanting it and crying loud enough to wake others. She winced and shrugged. "I'll need to change him first."

"I'll do it." He gave her the room keys, then reached into the diaper bag. He opened the back hatch and set Micah down on the flat surface. When the task was done, he lifted the little boy and nuzzled his soft, downy hair. The baby quieted against him, filling his heart with love.

"Shall we go inside?" Liz asked in a whisper.

He nodded, leading the way across the small parking lot to where their rooms were located. She used the key to access her room, then unlocked the connecting doors between the two.

He still needed to bring in the items from the SUV, but he was hesitant to set Micah down. Finally, he handed the baby to Liz so he could grab the rest of their things.

Once that was completed, he double-checked both locks on their respective doors.

"Sit down. I need to look at your arm." She went to work, opening the gauze packs and getting towels and a washcloth from the bathroom.

He sat patiently while she cleaned his wound. It hurt when she used hydrogen peroxide on it, but he didn't complain.

He was keenly aware of her sweet scent. Her nearness was distracting, and he had to remind himself she was an innocent victim here, just like Micah.

When she looked down at him, it was all he could do not to pull her close for a warm embrace. His cell phone vibrated, breaking the moment.

His voice was rough when he answered Wyatt's call. "Do you have information already?"

"Yeah, although you're not going to like it." Wyatt sounded as tired as he must have felt.

"Why is that?"

"Because the guy you shot is gone. Someone—maybe even the person who hired him—must have come back and scooped him up."

Agitated, Garrett rose to his feet, pacing the length of the room. "Are you sure you're in the right spot?"

"Yep." Wyatt sounded grim. "I found the blood and the flat tire you left behind, so I know this is the location of the shooting. Abby and I spread out and searched the woods to see if he was dragged and dumped. There's no sign of him."

Garrett's mind whirled. This didn't make any sense. Who had taken the dead man away?

And if there had been another gunman there, why hadn't they been shot and killed?

SIX

No dead body? Liz was close enough to Garrett to hear both sides of his conversation with Wyatt, but it was difficult to comprehend what he was saying.

"I checked for a pulse," Garrett said. "I know he was dead."

"I believe you. There's plenty of blood on the road." Wyatt's voice sounded strained. "You better be careful, boss. I don't like what's happening here."

"Yeah." Garrett caught her gaze. She offered a reassuring smile. "Thanks for checking in."

"Do you want us to contact the Brown County Sheriff's Department, anyway?" Wyatt asked.

Garrett considered this for a moment. "No. The report will only cause confusion. I need to think about what our next steps will be. I'm too tired to think clearly."

"Okay, we'll head back to Green Lake, then. But promise you'll call if you need us."

"Keep the county safe in my absence," Garrett said. "I'll call Liam in the morning to let him know I won't be in."

"We'll be okay. Abby and I can pull a double shift if needed," Wyatt offered.

She was impressed with how well the deputies supported Garrett. Their camaraderie made her realize how lonely her life had been since she'd buried herself in her clinic, caring for young mothers in need.

Maybe it was time to stop blaming herself for losing her daughter. Yet even as the thought flickered through her mind, she knew she couldn't.

Her husband had been right about the long hours impacting her pregnancy. She'd been too blind to notice. Until it was too late. Even though she'd lost Willow three years ago, she still remembered the moment she realized the baby had stopped moving.

Panic had gripped her by the throat, and by the time she'd gone in, it was too late.

"Take the deputy schedule up with Liam," Garrett said, interrupting her dark thoughts. "Thanks again for coming with a clean vehicle for us to use."

"Anytime. Later, boss." Wyatt disconnected from the call.

Liz forced herself to stay back from Garrett. His warmth called to her in way she didn't understand. She glanced at Micah, noticing he was squirming a bit as if about to wake up. He hadn't taken much of the bottle before Garrett had put him in a new diaper.

Obviously, that was about to change.

"Hey there," she crooned, picking Micah up. "Are you awake?" His dark eyes blinked up at her, making her smile. "Oh, yes, you are. And hungry, too, hmm?"

"I can feed him," Garrett offered.

She hesitated, then handed the infant over to him. This was what she'd wanted—for Garrett to bond with his son. So why did she feel let down? She turned away and rummaged in the bag for the bottle she'd made just a few minutes ago.

Garrett lowered himself into the single chair in the corner of the room, giving Micah the bottle. She took the free time to slip into the bathroom to clean up.

Thanks to their trek through the woods, her hair was tangled with leaves and other debris. Using her fingers, she combed through the long dark strands, dropping pine needles and bits of leaves and sticks in the garbage can. Then she splashed cold water on her face.

She reminded herself that it was a good sign that Garrett was taking over caring for his baby. She was happy for them, as the little guy needed his father now more than ever. Not only had he lost his mother, but there were multiple determined gunmen tracking them. Yet she had the utmost confidence that Garrett would do everything possible to keep his son safe.

Feeling better, she emerged from the bathroom. The chair in which Garrett had been sitting was empty, but she heard him murmuring to the baby through the connecting doorway of their rooms. He'd also taken the diaper bag with him, making her feel even more useless.

After crossing the room, she hovered in the doorway. "Everything okay?"

He glanced up in surprise. "Yes. I only moved to give you privacy. You must be exhausted, too. Besides, Micah is my responsibility, not yours."

It was on the tip of her tongue to remind him how he'd begged for her help when she first arrived, but she managed to hold back. She had to admire his determination to do his part. However, most young babies benefited from having two parents.

"I know Micah is your responsibility, but I also need you alert and focused on keeping us safe. Don't forget, I'm here to help."

His expression softened. "I appreciate that very much.

And I promise I will wake you if needed. For now, try to get some rest."

"I will if you do the same." She smiled, then partially closed the door on her side. Not to shut him out, but to give him privacy, too.

After she'd crawled into bed, she found herself staring blindly up at the ceiling, wishing for something she could never have.

A family of her own.

Liz hadn't expected to fall asleep, but the sound of a baby crying jerked her from slumber. She bolted out of bed and hurried over the threshold to care for Micah. Garrett groaned and lifted his head. "I can get him."

"You need more sleep. I'll take a turn." Cradling the baby in her arms, she took the diaper bag into her room, using her hip to close the connecting door so that Garrett could fall back to sleep.

She truly didn't mind changing Micah and then making another bottle for him. The baby instantly quieted as she fed him, his dark gaze clinging to hers.

"You are so very precious," she whispered, her heart full of love for this tiny baby. "And I'm very glad you seem to be eating well." Up until now, it hadn't bothered her that she'd taken Micah directly to Garrett without having a doctor examine him. At the time, she'd been more concerned about his safety. Not to mention, women had been delivering children on their own for years without having a doctor in attendance.

But Micah should be seen by a pediatrician, and soon. Her expertise was delivering babies and caring for new mothers postdelivery. Her clinical practice didn't include follow-up appointments related to an infant's ongoing health.

Her thoughts turned to Rebecca. In reviewing her steps

upon Rebecca's arrival, she couldn't come up with anything else she could have done to save the young woman's life. Especially not after she'd placed the needle to relieve her acute tension pneumothorax.

Still, the events of that night, followed by the subsequent gunfire, was troubling. She clutched Micah close. Garrett would protect them, and he knew she'd do the same. Protect this innocent child with her own life, if necessary.

The way any mother would.

Garrett must have fallen back to sleep, because when he awoke, bright sunlight streamed in through the motel-room windows. He sat up, running his hand through his dark brown hair. He'd stayed up with Micah for too long, but he couldn't deny the sheer wonder at how he and Rebecca had created the beautiful baby.

He still felt guilty about spending the night with Rebecca, but having Micah softened the edges, making him realize how blessed he was to have a son.

After washing up in the bathroom, he took a minute to call Sheriff Liam Harland. His boss answered on the first ring.

"Harland."

"It's Garrett. I'm sorry to say I need a short leave of absence." He thought about how much to tell him, then decided it was best to come all the way clean. "I have a son, Liam. And his mother was shot right before she gave birth. She didn't make it, but the gunmen showed up at the sheriff's department and then again at my house. I need to keep Micah and the midwife who delivered him safe."

"A son? Congrats!" Trust Liam to look on the bright side first. "I'm sorry to hear about the gunmen, though. And the loss of the baby's mother. What can I do to help?"

He was humbled by Liam's willingness to pitch in. "We're safe now, so all I need is time off. To figure out what's going on and to bond with my son."

"Of course. That's a given. Take as much time as you need," Liam assured him. "And know this—we're here for you. It doesn't matter that this is our busy time. You're family. We'll do whatever we can to support you."

"Thanks." He was blessed to have Liam as his boss. "I'll be in touch soon."

"Okay, take care." Liam ended the call.

After pocketing his phone, he turned toward the connecting doorway. The power bar he'd eaten in the middle of the night was long gone, and his stomach rumbled with hunger. Peeking into Liz's room, he found her sleeping in the chair, Micah on the floor beside her.

She was so beautiful, he had to force himself to focus his attention on his son. Last night, he'd been determined not to take advantage of Liz's kindness. But when she'd come to take Micah, he'd gratefully let her feed him so he could get more badly needed sleep.

How did single parents do it? These past twenty-four hours had made him realize how difficult some people had it.

It was humbling to know God had blessed him with this baby. He made a silent promise not to disappoint Him— and that meant letting go of his anger over Jason's untimely death.

And some of his own guilt, too.

"Good morning." Liz's husky voice drew his gaze from his son. Her smile sent his pulse into high gear.

"Good morning." He cleared his throat, hoping to sound normal. "I appreciate you letting me sleep in."

"Of course." She glanced at Micah, then stood. "How long can we stay here?"

"Checkout time is eleven. We have two hours." He frowned. "I would feel better if we moved on to a new location after we grab something to eat."

"Okay." She didn't argue his proposed plan. She stretched, then added, "I would love breakfast."

He grinned. "A woman after my own heart. Should we wait until Micah wakes up?"

"No need. He should sleep for at least another hour or so." She waved a hand. "We'll have his diaper bag with us if he wakes earlier."

He bowed to her expertise. "Okay, let's hit the road. There's a family-style restaurant across the street."

"Sounds perfect." She bent to grab the diaper bag. "First, though, I'd like to look at your arm."

He glanced at the gauze she'd wrapped around his injury. "It's fine. Trust me, I would let you know if it felt worse."

Scowling, she planted her hands on her hips. "I'd rather make sure there isn't an infection before it settles in your bloodstream."

Resigning himself to the inevitable, he gestured for her to come into his room, where they were less likely to disturb Micah. As before, she took a moment to spread out her supplies, including a washcloth and the hydrogen peroxide, then unwrapped the gauze. As she worked, he craned his neck to see the wound for himself.

To his inexpert eye, it looked fine. She pressed on his skin around the injury, then proceeded to wash and redress it.

"Told you it was fine," he grumbled.

"And I still think you could use a few doses of antibiotics," she shot back. "Didn't we pass a sign for a medical center on the way in?"

"I'm not going," he said firmly. "Gunshot wounds are an automatic report to the police, and that will only open a can of worms." He frowned. "However, it might be smart to take Micah in to be checked out. Don't most babies see a doctor after they're born?"

"Yes. I had the same thought, but we can't just walk into the emergency department when there isn't anything wrong with him." She grimaced. "The emergency-department doctor would simply refer you to a pediatrician, anyway. They're not set up to perform well-baby visits."

"I guess that settles it." He stood and flexed his arm, glad it wasn't his shooting hand. The pain was negligible and wouldn't hold him back from keeping them safe. "No point in stopping in at the medical center."

She sighed but let it go. He thought about the computer, but he was too hungry to spend time searching for Rebecca's relatives now.

Food first; then he'd tackle their next steps. What he really wanted was to contact Rebecca's father. If the guy was still well enough to communicate, he hoped to convince him to take Micah out of the line of succession for the inheritance. A college fund or something similar would be more than enough.

He could provide for his son. They didn't need the headache of fighting heirs over the Woodward fortune. That kind of money didn't buy happiness.

In fact, he felt certain it was just the opposite. Rebecca had claimed the summers she'd spent in Green Lake had been the best of her life. Nights spent sitting at the edge of the lake or stealing a kiss at the campfire...

No, that kind of money wasn't worth it.

Pushing those troublesome thoughts aside, he put the laptop strap over his shoulder. He peered through the window, scanning the parking lot, before carrying Micah outside. Liz followed close behind with the diaper bag.

The bright day without a cloud in the sky promised warm summer temperatures. Normally, he'd be concerned about tourists causing trouble out on Green Lake. But there wasn't anything he could do, now that he was on a leave of absence.

The family restaurant wasn't as busy as he'd anticipated. They were taken to a booth in the corner. He tucked Micah's carrier in beside him.

A server arrived with coffee. When their mugs were full, they perused the menu, then placed their orders.

"This seems like a nice town," Liz commented before sipping her coffee. "It feels as if nothing bad could happen here."

He'd once thought the same thing about Green Lake, until he'd gone into law enforcement. Liam's wife, Shauna, had been in danger; then some of the Amish members of the community had danger show up on their doorstep, too. Now this. He shook his head. "Unfortunately, bad things can happen anywhere."

"True." She lowered her mug. "Where are we going next?"

It was a good question. "We could push on through to La Cross. It's about thirty miles west of here. Or we could turn and head south to Madison." He shrugged. "La Cross is closer."

"I'd prefer La Cross—although I don't know how we're going to figure out who hired the gunmen."

He wasn't sure about that himself. He sat back as their server arrived with their food. When she left, Liz leaned forward to take his hand. "We should say grace."

Squeezing her hand, he bowed his head. It had been a long time since he'd done this, but the prayer came easily. "Dear Lord, we thank You for this wonderful food and keeping us safe in Your care. Amen."

"Amen," Liz whispered.

He wanted to savor the moment, but Micah began wiggling in his carrier. He quickly dove into his meal, eating in record time so he could tend to his son.

"I'll make him a bottle in the restroom," Liz offered, scooting out of her seat.

Micah was awake but hadn't started crying yet. He blinked in the light as if wondering where he was, but Garrett knew it wouldn't take long for him to fuss. He lifted the boy from his carrier and held him with his injured arm while trying to finish his breakfast with the other.

Micah's tiny face crumpled just as Liz returned. Garrett flashed a smile as he quickly gave his son the bottle. "Just in time."

"I'll take him," she offered.

"He's fine. I'm just about finished, anyway." He ate the last slice of crispy bacon, then pushed his plate aside. "I'd like to call Rebecca's father sooner than later, though. Maybe we can stop by the motel long enough to use the internet so I can look up the best way to try to contact him."

"Okay, but I don't think billionaires list their personal phone numbers on the web," she said.

"I know. But there would be a phone number for his company, and I might be able to get through to someone by using Rebecca's name." It was the only idea he could come up with.

"Hang on." She pulled out her phone, then nodded. "There's internet here. Give me Micah, I'll hold him while you log on."

He did as she asked, passing the baby across the table. He couldn't help but smile at how Liz cooed over his son. Turning his attention to more important issues, he opened the laptop and connected to the free Wi-fi.

It was slow, but it worked well enough for him to find the corporate offices of Woodward Enterprises. He started with the general number, letting the assistant who answered the phone know that he had important information related to Rebecca and her baby that he needed to give to Robert Woodward.

"Hold on, please." Before he could agree, there was nothing but dead air. He waited three full minutes before another voice answered.

"This is Edward Woodward's assistant," a pleasant voice said. "How may I help you?"

Edward was Robert's younger brother—and a suspect, along with his children, Elaine and Jeremy. "I don't want to speak to Edward. I need to talk to Robert directly."

"I'm sorry, that's not an option. He's been moved into hospice care. Edward is in charge now, and he would be happy to help in any way he can."

Hospice care. The news shouldn't have been a shock. "I'm sorry. That won't work. Goodbye." He quickly disconnected, then powered down the phone in case they decided to try tracing the call.

"What is it?" Liz's expression reflected her concern.

"Edward Woodward is in charge," he said. "And Rebecca's father has been moved into hospice."

"Oh, no. That's so sad."

Did Robert even know about Rebecca's death? He thought it was interesting Edward's assistant hadn't asked more questions about Rebecca or her baby.

He decided to call the dispatcher to find out if either Wyatt or Abby were still on duty. A horrible thought had occurred to him, and he needed more information—fast.

"Wyatt is on his way home. Would you like me to connect you?"

"Please." There was a pause before Wyatt answered.

"Hey. I need you to call the Brown County morgue to see if Rebecca's body has been taken there."

"Okay. I'll call you right back." Wyatt clicked off, presumably to make the call. He had a bad feeling about this.

It took almost ten minutes for Wyatt to call back. He put the call on speaker for Liz to hear, too. "No female Jane Doe or Rebecca Woodward has been taken to the Brown County Medical Examiner's office or to the local hospital."

That was exactly what he'd been afraid of. "These guys are getting rid of the bodies to eliminate any evidence."

"Yep," Wyatt agreed. "No body, no crime. At least, it's much harder to prove there was a crime. Are you guys okay? Do you need us to come back you up?"

"No thanks. Go home and get some sleep." He disconnected from the call, then powered down his phone. "Make sure to keep yours off from this point forward, too," he instructed.

Eyes wide, she nodded.

He stared out the window. Rebecca's body had been taken away, just like the gunman he'd shot in self-defense.

The situation had gone from bad to worse. And despite his years on the job, he wasn't sure what to do about it.

SEVEN

Liz swallowed hard, wishing she hadn't left Rebecca's body behind in her clinic. Yet she'd needed to keep Micah safe and had called the ambulance to respond to Rebecca's death. How had the gunmen found Rebecca's body prior to the ambulance arriving?

They must have been closer than she'd realized. And one had followed her to the sheriff's department.

Her distress must have been evident, because Garrett reached over to take her hand. "Please don't be upset. It's not your fault."

"I keep trying to tell myself that." She shook her head, feeling helpless. "I only left because of the potential danger to Micah. And that has been proven to be a bigger concern than I realized." She held his gaze. "It's all surreal."

"You have that right." He gently squeezed her hand. "We'll need to pick up disposable phones and continue staying off-grid as much as possible."

"I understand." She gazed at Micah's sleeping face, knowing just how lost she'd be without Garrett's support. Based on everything that had transpired, returning to her clinic wasn't an option.

What if she could never go back? A surge of panic tightened her chest. She couldn't abandon her patients. They needed her!

Then again, so did Micah—at least for now, while Garrett searched for the bad guys.

She struggled to breathe normally, letting go of her fears. Her future was in God's hands.

Their server returned with more coffee, smiling at Micah. "He's so precious. What's his name?"

"Micah," she and Garrett answered at the exact same time.

Their server laughed as she finished filling their mugs. "It's always nice to see a beautiful family."

Her gaze clashed with Garrett's, a flush creeping over her cheeks, but neither of them corrected her assumption. Garrett smiled softly, then turned his attention back to the laptop.

"If you don't mind, I'd like to stay here for another few minutes." His fingers worked the keyboard. "I need to see if there are other possible heirs who should be considered suspects."

"Anything that helps us get to the bottom of this mess is fine with me." It still boggled her mind to think that anyone would kill an innocent baby over money.

She glanced around the restaurant, enjoying the cheerful atmosphere. The family-friendly place seemed safe, far away from the gunmen who stalked them.

"I need to make a list," Garrett muttered.

"A list about what?"

"Heirs to the Woodward fortune if Micah was out of the picture." He frowned. "Robert's brother, Edward, has two kids, Elaine and Jeremy. But now it looks like Robert has a sister, too—Connie. And her daughter, Anita."

"Edward, Elaine, Jeremy, Connie and Anita," she repeated, to memorize their names. "Would the inheritance be split between them evenly? Or would one sibling get more than the others?"

"That's a good question—although, from searching the website, it appears both Edward and Connie Malone, which is her married name, work in the business. They must report to Rebecca, who was named CEO a few months ago, which is when Robert declared her and her baby the heir to his company." He grimaced. "It's possible with her and Micah gone, they'd have equal shares, along with their children. If that's the case, Edward has the advantage."

She shifted her gaze to the sleeping infant. "Rebecca was CEO, huh? He must have given her that role right after he learned about his cancer. I'm not a cancer expert, but being diagnosed with stage four pancreatic cancer usually means a life expectancy of nine months to a year at the most."

"I think Rebecca was always slated to take over, but the timing may have been pushed up because of his diagnosis," Garrett agreed thoughtfully. "I wonder how her aunt and uncle feel about reporting to her. Although, that's not a problem any longer."

"Maybe that's part of the reason she was in danger." Remembering the fear in Rebecca's eyes made her shiver. "Are we sure Micah is the sole heir? That's a lot of pressure to put on one person. You mentioned an article, but maybe Robert's will names others, too."

"That gives me an idea." He went back to the keyboard. "Maybe there's a way to speak to Robert's lawyer."

"It would be nice if he could put us in touch with Robert directly." She brightened at the possibility. "There's still time for him to change his will."

"It's possible." Garrett sighed. "Trust me, I'd love nothing more than to get the target off my son's back. However, I would think the rest of the family would have tried to convince him to change the will by now if that was possible."

She hated to admit he was right. "Rebecca sought help in

my clinic for a reason," she murmured. "The note you found in her car indicates she came all this way to have her baby in a location no one would find her."

"Except they did find her." He raked his hand over his face. "I really wish she'd have called me beforehand. I could have been there for her. I could have kept her safe."

"I guess we shouldn't keep playing the what-if game." She sighed. "Rebecca must have had her reasons."

"Maybe." He scowled at the screen, not looking convinced. "There's nothing on the Woodward Enterprises website that mentions a lawyer."

Their server came over one more time to refill their mugs and leave their bill. Since the restaurant seemed to be filling up with people, Liz gestured to the receipt. "We should leave, let others have the table."

"Okay." Garrett closed the computer and stuffed it back in the case. He paid the tab, then waited as she strapped Micah into his seat. He carried the baby through the restaurant and headed outside.

As always, he scanned the area as they walked to the SUV. She was certain they were safe here, but she appreciated how he stayed alert.

It took a few minutes for them to get situated, and as Garrett drove out of the parking lot, pausing to turn right to head into town, she noticed a black SUV with tinted windows pull up to the motel.

"Garrett?" She reached out to grasp his arm as he made the turn. "Quick! Look at that SUV."

He glanced over, his expression turning grim as he continued driving down the road, away from the motel. "Did you get the license plate?"

"No, sorry." She twisted in her seat, trying to see better.

Two men climbed out of the vehicle. "There's two of them," she whispered. "I can't see anything more."

"Two men?" he echoed.

She nodded, clasping her trembling fingers together. "It could be nothing, right? Just a couple of guys scouting the area, looking for a place to stay?"

"I doubt it." His gaze was glued to the rearview mirror. "We should have left the restaurant right away, rather than staying to use the internet."

She gaped at him. "You think they traced the internet connection?"

"No. They'd have come straight to the restaurant." She noticed he didn't speed or try to be conspicuous as he turned left at the intersection and drove through a suburban neighborhood. Her heart pounded with fear, but she tried to remain calm. The houses were quaint, and many had beautiful flower gardens out front. It would be a great place to stay, except for the black SUV with tinted windows back at the motel.

"How did they find us?"

He glanced at her. "They could have tracked our phones prior to our turning them off."

If that was true, she wished they'd shut them off earlier. As Garrett continued making his way through town, she thought about the two men who were determined to find them.

She and Garrett were the only thing standing between the gunmen and Micah. To hurt the baby, they'd have to kill them first.

She could only hope and pray it wouldn't come to that.

Kicking himself for being complacent, Garrett managed to wind his way through town to the other side of Viroqua.

He took the highway south, deciding against going to La Cross. Since these guys had shown up here, he figured it was better to backtrack a bit, hoping they wouldn't anticipate that.

So much for finding a peaceful place to stay off-grid.

Tracking their phones was the only way they could have found them here. The gunmen seemed to have unlimited resources at their disposal. Far more than he did.

He told himself he was a cop with years of experience behind him. Surely he could outsmart these guys.

But not if he didn't keep his mind focused on their safety. Staying at the restaurant for so long had been a rookie mistake.

And he couldn't afford to make another.

"I thought we were going to La Cross?"

"Not anymore." He continued keeping a wary eye on the rearview mirror. The fact that they hadn't shown up at the restaurant was only slightly reassuring. He didn't believe they knew what car he was driving.

Keeping his speed near the speed limit as to not draw undue attention wasn't easy. He wanted to hit the gas and speed far away from the threat.

"Where are we going?" Liz asked, her voice low.

"I don't know yet." He tried to envision a map of Central Wisconsin in his mind. He didn't necessarily want to head to Madison, but Green Lake wasn't an option, either.

Should they drive all the way to Chicago? That would take the entire day, and even if he showed up at the office building that housed Woodward Enterprises, he doubted he'd get very far.

And the thought of taking Micah anywhere near the company his mother ran as CEO made him feel sick to his stomach. Rebecca had claimed to love working for her father; she'd thrived on the responsibility.

A decision that may have cost her life.

Not that it was her fault she had greedy relatives. He wondered what Joel had to say about that.

Wait a minute. He looked at the laptop computer he'd set on the floor of the front seat. "Joel," he said. "I should have thought about Joel."

"Who?" Liz looked confused.

"The last time I saw Rebecca, she mentioned a guy she'd hired as her chief financial officer. A man named Joel Abernathy." Had the guy been listed on the website? He had been so focused on identifying the potential heirs that he hadn't looked at the hierarchy of the company's leadership team.

"What about him?" Liz frowned. "I don't see how a CFO would be a possible heir to the estate."

He tried to put his feelings into words. "I was upset over losing a young cop in the line of duty during the time Rebecca came to visit. That night…" He flushed and forced himself to continue. "I let my emotions cloud my judgment. We spent the night together, and I have to assume that's when Micah was conceived."

"I'm sorry you lost a young officer." Liz rested her hand on his arm. "I'm sure that was difficult for you—and you don't have to explain your personal life to me. I'm still not getting how Joel is a part of this, though."

He wasn't doing a good job of explaining. "I wanted Rebecca to stay in Green Lake, to give a relationship between us a try. She told me as much as she enjoyed spending time here, she couldn't give up her role with the company. She mentioned she'd been spending a lot of time with Joel, their new hire. At the time, I assumed she meant they were spending time together as professionals. But when I called a few weeks later, she told me she was seeing someone else."

"And you think that someone was Joel?" Her gaze was skeptical. "She could have been seeing anyone."

"True." He couldn't deny the possibility he was making a big deal out of nothing. "But what if she wasn't? What if she'd gotten close to Joel, then decided to date him?"

"After spending the night with you?" The way Liz said the words indicated she didn't think much of Rebecca's decision. "Why would she lead you on like that?"

"She didn't—not really." He glanced in the rearview mirror again, noticing there were a few cars on the highway behind him. They were too far away to make out whether they were SUVs with tinted windows, though. "We were friends for years. I cared for her, a lot. I thought she felt the same way, especially when we spent the night together. But maybe she ultimately regretted what we'd done."

Liz opened her mouth as if to argue, but she must have changed her mind. After a moment, she said, "Okay, so when we find a safe place and have the chance to get disposable phones, you should reach out to Joel. See what he has to say."

"I will." It felt good to have a goal. Now, if he could just come up with a destination… A sign loomed ahead, indicating the small town of Readsville was ten miles away. He pointed at it. "Keep your eyes open for any motel signs. I'm not sure if Readsville is big enough to have one or not. It looks pretty rustic out here."

"Okay." She flashed a wry smile. "I bet they have a library. *Reads*ville? Get it?"

He chuckled at her weak joke. "That would be nice, but I'd rather have a motel that takes cash and a place we can get carryout food." No more going to restaurants where they would be sitting ducks.

He looked at the cars behind him again. The closest vehicle was moving faster now, narrowing the gap between them. He tightened his grip on the steering wheel, trying to decide if the vehicle posed a threat or if he was letting his imagination run wild.

The car kept coming. Since they were on a narrow single-lane highway, he slowed and moved over onto the shoulder, hoping the driver would pass.

He didn't.

Highway Junction JJ loomed in his line of sight. He hit the brake and wrenched the wheel, taking the sharp right-hand turn. Then he punched the gas, desperate to put distance between them and the car following.

"What's going on?" Liz grabbed her armrest and twisted in her seat. "Did the tinted SUV find us?"

He didn't answer, mostly because he was desperately searching for a place where they could hide out. He hated the idea of risking Micah's safety during a high-speed car chase.

Although he would if he had no other choice.

"I don't understand. How did they catch up? We don't have our phones on!" Liz's voice rose in alarm.

"Hang on." The car tracking them had managed to make the turn, too, although the driver had lost some ground. Within seconds, the vehicle was out of view. This highway was even narrower than the one they'd left, and it was curvy, too. He seriously needed to figure out a way to lose their tail.

"Call 911. Let them know a black car is following us on Highway Double J." He went as fast as possible on the curvy road—which was no easy feat, since he couldn't see what was up ahead. He wished he had his phone so he could use the GPS. From what he could tell, there were no other intersections in sight, not even a driveway leading to a lone house.

He went several miles as Liz spoke to the dispatcher,

explaining the danger and trying to give clues as to where they were located. Even as he heard her use the highway markers as identifiers, he feared any police response would be too late.

Please, Lord, guide us to safety!

When Liz glanced at him, he realized he'd whispered the prayer out loud.

There! He caught a glimpse of a small house partially hidden in the trees. He hit the brake hard, scanning the side of the road for a driveway.

There was a narrow opening between the trees, with gravel covering the ground. He hesitated, not wanting to put others in danger, but then he turned into the driveway, going up far enough for the trees on either side to give them cover—and hoping they weren't visible from the house, either.

"We're just going to sit here?" Liz asked.

"No, we're getting out. I'll take Micah. You grab the laptop case and diaper bag. Please, hurry. We need to be far away before the vehicle passes this driveway."

Liz jumped into action, grabbing the laptop and pushing her door open in one quick movement. By the time he'd unbuckled Micah's carrier, she had the diaper bag, too.

"Follow me." He'd noticed the small wooded area was slightly more dense to the right of the vehicle. He headed that way, hoping and praying the owner of the property wouldn't come down and demand to know what they were doing.

To his surprise, there was a small woodpile—cut logs that were neatly stacked between two trees offering some semblance of cover. They were a little too close to the open area leading up to the house for comfort, but it was the best protection they could ask for.

Liz didn't protest when he headed toward the woodpile.

Rounding the tree at one end, he set Micah's carrier down, then gestured for her to crouch beside him.

"Stay down," he whispered. Then he pulled out his weapon and hunkered down beside her. He moved two of the logs so that he'd have a better view of the trail leading from their car.

The trees were thick enough that he could barely see the road. He alternated between looking at the road and the path ahead of them.

The area was so quiet, he could easily hear the car engine approaching. Liz huddled over Micah, using her body as a shield. It humbled him to know she'd risk her life for his son.

A car moved down the road before slowing to a stop. He held his breath, then forced himself to breathe as the vehicle backed up.

Keep going, he silently pleaded. *Keep going!*

The seconds passed with agonizing slowness. No doubt the driver of the vehicle was trying to decide if they'd turned off or not.

Keep going!

As if in answer to his silent plea, the car rolled past, gaining speed.

Still, he didn't move. This could be nothing more than a trap to draw them out of hiding. They were stuck here until he was convinced the gunmen were gone.

EIGHT

Silently praying, Liz covered Micah's body with her own. She trusted Garrett's cop instincts. If he thought the gunmen would return to find them, then she believed him.

For ten long minutes, she heard nothing. But then the barest rumble of a car engine reached her ears. Lifting her head, she reached out to touch Garrett's arm.

With a grim look, he nodded in understanding. He'd heard it, too.

The gunmen? Or someone else? Her heart thudded loudly in her ears as she strained to listen.

The sound of the car engine grew louder. From where she was positioned, huddling over Micah and tucked behind the wood stack, she couldn't see anything.

She felt Garrett tense beside her and knew something was going on. Then the car engine abruptly went silent. Garrett put a finger to his lips, indicating she shouldn't talk, then tucked the SUV key fob into her hands. His intense blue gaze implored her to get Micah to safety if anything should happen to him.

Please, Lord Jesus, keep us safe! Grant Garrett the strength and wisdom he needs to fight these men!

Taking a long, deep breath on the heels of her desperate prayer helped calm her racing heart. She couldn't hear anything else now but could easily imagine the gunmen spreading out to search for them.

A rustling sound almost made her gasp. She continued protecting Micah's body with hers, ignoring the urge to run from danger.

Then Micah began to cry. *No! Not now!*

A sharp retort of gunfire reverberated around them. Garrett must have been watching the guy approach, because he fired back a fraction of a second later. The sound of a man's cry, loud enough to be heard over Micah's fussing, indicated he'd hit his mark.

Another gunshot echoed through the trees. Had the second man come to back up the first? Garrett returned fire, only this time there was no sound of an injury. Or maybe she just couldn't hear it, as Micah's cries were growing louder.

She glanced helplessly up at Garrett, but he was focused on the scene beyond the woodpile. Biting her lip, she considered her options. She had the diaper bag, and there was still some premade formula in the can she'd used the previous day—but it hadn't been refrigerated, and she wouldn't dare offer that to a one-day old baby. There was another can in the bag. She wasn't sure there was time to make another bottle. Not if they had to take off at a run.

Dragging the bag toward her, she found the pacifier, hoping the baby would take it. Micah accepted the rubber tip but then must have realized he wasn't getting any food, because he spat it back out.

Garrett gave her a reassuring look, then eased out from behind the woodpile. She wanted to call him back, but she stayed where she was. Had he injured both men? It seemed wrong to pray that he had. Yet she wanted Micah to be safe.

And men stalking them with guns was anything but.

She picked Micah up, holding him against her shoulder

to soothe him. He quieted a bit, but it didn't last long. She wanted to look over the top of the logs, but she didn't dare expose herself or the baby to more gunfire.

After what seemed like an eternity, Garrett came back. "One man down. The other took off. I think I wounded him—there's a spot of blood where he'd been standing."

"We're safe?"

"For now." She should have known their safety was only temporary. "Get Micah into the SUV. I'm calling for backup. This time, the dead guy isn't going anywhere but to the closest morgue."

"Okay." She gently tucked the crying baby into the carrier and hauled him, the laptop and the diaper bag back to the SUV. She passed by a gunman lying face up on the ground between two trees.

She felt terrible for Garrett. This was the second time he'd been forced to kill to keep them safe. Granted, he'd only done so in self-defense, but she felt certain he didn't treat taking a life lightly.

She didn't, either. Why couldn't these gunmen just go away and leave them alone?

Upon reaching the car, she took the time to buckle Micah's carrier into place before crawling in beside him to make the bottle. She wasn't sure if they'd have to hit the road again soon but was determined to be prepared.

Micah's cries subsided when she offered him a fresh bottle. She sighed in relief, realizing they'd need to stock up on supplies very soon. She'd used the last can of premade formula. They needed more if they found themselves in a similar situation.

Though she hoped they wouldn't have to keep hiding from assailants for much longer.

Glancing out the window, she noticed an older man standing several feet from Garrett, his expression set in a deep scowl. The homeowner, no doubt. And she didn't blame the man for being upset over what had taken place on his property.

Garrett had his badge out and was gesturing to the area behind him, likely explaining what had happened. The guy kept his distance, as if wary about Garrett's story.

The wail of police sirens was a welcome relief. She wondered if the cop was responding to her initial call or to the homeowner, who'd likely called in the shots fired.

Either way, she was glad they weren't in this alone. Micah's gaze held hers, and her heart squeezed with love and the realization of how close they'd been to getting hurt.

Or worse.

Two police cars pulled into the driveway behind the SUV. Garrett had his hands up where they could be seen, holding his badge in one of them as he jogged over.

The homeowner stayed back, watching from afar.

Micah was still drinking his bottle when the officers emerged from their squads with their guns drawn. She could hear Garrett through the closed windows.

"I'm Chief Deputy Garrett Nichols from the Green Lake County Sheriff's Department." He continued holding his hands palm forward, showing them the badge. "Two gunmen trailed us here. They initiated the shooting. I fired back in self-defense. One gunman is down. The other is wounded but took off."

"Who's in the SUV?" one of them shouted.

"Liz Templeton and my son, Micah. We're all in danger. The gunmen have been tracking us for the past twenty-four hours."

She watched as one of the officers used his radio to talk to someone. Both officers stayed alert until they'd received a response. Then they slowly lowered and holstered their weapons.

Garrett lowered his hands, too, but didn't put his badge away. Micah finished his bottle, so she held him up against her shoulder to burp him. Then she opened the door to step out of the car with the baby.

"You have to understand, we're in danger," she said.

"And you're Liz Templeton?" the taller of the two officers asked. "Lizbeth Templeton?"

The way he used her full name indicated he'd had her run through their system. Likely Garrett's, too. She nodded. "I'm a witness to the shooting incident. We tried to hide from the gunmen on this man's property, but they came back and began searching for us. When the baby started crying, the gunmen found us. That's when Garrett returned fire."

Maybe it was Micah's presence there, but the officers seemed to believe her.

The homeowner came down to discuss the situation, too. It took longer than she'd have liked to give their statements and to ensure the dead man was taken to the Volver County morgue.

A solid two hours later, she and Garrett were allowed to leave. She found herself hesitant to part from the relative safety of the officers behind.

"Now what?" she asked, clicking her seat belt into place.

"We need to get to a motel and make arrangements with Liam to swap this for another vehicle." Garrett looked exhausted, as if the shooting had drained his energy.

"Another car?"

"The wounded man who got away could have this license plate." He raked his hand through his dark chestnut hair. "I wish we could head back to Green Lake, but I think we're better off in a different city—hopefully one that will enable us to go off-grid."

"That hasn't worked so far," she murmured.

"No, it hasn't." He looked completely dejected. She rested her hand on his arm.

"I knew you would keep us safe, Garrett. God is watching over us."

He glanced at her and nodded, though she didn't think he believed her.

But the cops who had arrived at the scene had. And she knew Liam probably did, too. All she could do was continue to pray for this nightmare to end.

Very soon.

Garrett was keenly aware of Liz's soft hand on his arm. As much as he felt bad about killing a man, he was glad they had a body for evidence. The officers who'd responded had agreed to keep him in the loop on the guy's identity.

They needed something to go on, some clue to link back to the person who'd hired these guys. The way the assailants had found them again was unnerving. Was it possible they'd chosen the same route he had by accident?

Or did they have more help and resources than he realized?

The thought of having access to cop-like resources was sobering. Either way, he needed a better plan. And maybe being out in the middle of nowhere was working against them. He'd originally intended to stay south, but now he embraced the idea of heading northeast toward Portage, the city that housed the state prison. It wasn't a large city like Milwaukee or Madison, but it was big enough for them to get lost in, or so he hoped. And there were plenty of transient people there, too.

They needed to buy replacement phones ASAP. The urge to call Liam was strong, but he wouldn't risk using their personal phones.

He turned north at the next highway, one that was even smaller than the one they had been on. Liz was unusually quiet. "You okay?"

"Yes. But I lost ten years off my life when Micah woke up crying when the gunmen were out there."

He grimaced. "I know, but it worked in our favor. The sound startled the guy who was closest to me. He lashed out, firing almost at random without looking." The exchange had been hairy, but in the end, they'd prevailed. "The good news is that we'll soon have an ID on this guy, if he's in the system."

"And if he's not?"

He sighed. "That's possible, but I don't think your average citizen accepts a job like this. It takes someone with a cold heart to kill a baby. It's more likely the perp has a criminal background already."

"That makes sense." She turned to look back at Micah sleeping in his seat. "That was a close one, Garrett. If something had happened to you, I don't think Micah would have survived."

"I know. We can't let them get that close again." At least they hadn't stayed in the car, where they would have easily been found.

They rode in silence for the next hour. He was slightly reassured to see there were no vehicles on this deserted stretch of highway, but he knew that would change once they came closer to their destination. Despite their full breakfast, his stomach rumbled with hunger, so he searched for restaurant signs. There were several to pick from once they reached the town of Portage. The large prison, surrounded by high fences topped with barbed wire, could be seen from the road as they approached. It made him think about how many guys he and Liam and the other deputies had arrested and ultimately sent there to serve their sentences.

Not as many as those arrested in the bigger cities, but they had seen an increase in crime in their small town.

And that danger had returned tenfold.

Their first stop was at a store that sold phones and other supplies. Liz looked relieved to have the chance to stock up on items for Micah.

By the time they'd finished, his stomach was growling in earnest. Checking his watch, he figured they had time to eat before his son awoke.

He considered ordering takeout, but he discovered the restaurant was on Main Street and the parking lot for all the businesses was two blocks away. Hoping they'd be safe enough for now, he requested a booth in the back of the restaurant that was closest to the kitchen so they'd have an escape route if needed.

"Everything looks good," Liz said as she perused the menu. "I don't know why I'm so hungry when all we did was sit in the car for hours."

"Being hit with an adrenaline rush works up an appetite." He'd experienced that before. "I noticed there were several hotels here, too. We'll see if we can get another set of connecting rooms after lunch."

"That would be nice."

When their meal arrived, he decided to take the lead on saying grace. God had watched over them today, and he knew how much he needed Him to get through this. Reaching across the table, he took Liz's hand. "Dear Lord Jesus, thank You for keeping us safe today. We ask for Your continued guidance and wisdom as we seek those who wish us harm. Amen."

"Amen." Liz lifted her gaze. "That was beautiful, Garrett."

He nodded, feeling self-conscious. "I know you said God was always there for me, and I believe that's true. I should not have turned my back on Him after Jason's death."

"We're all human, and we make mistakes." She munched on a french fry, then added, "When I lost my daughter as a stillborn, then found my husband in the arms of another woman, I went through the same anger toward God as you did. It wasn't easy to understand why God took my daughter." She glanced at Micah, a soft smile tugging at her lips. "Then I began helping low-income women living on and off the reservation and began to see how He wanted me to use my talents and my experience to help others."

"I didn't know about your daughter and husband. I'm so sorry." He marveled at her ability to put her anger aside.

"Thank you. It's been hard, especially after Eric's death, but I'm in a better place now."

Even with the gunmen on their tail? That was even more humbling. "I believe God sent Rebecca to you for Micah's sake. And I'm very glad you brought him to me."

"Me, too."

It wasn't fair that her life was in danger, and for a moment, he considered taking Micah far away, changing their names and dropping out of sight.

But he sensed the person behind this wouldn't rest until he or she knew the heir wasn't a threat.

Besides, he wouldn't walk away from Liz or force her to go away with him and Micah. No, the only way out of this was to find the person responsible and have them arrested.

With a renewed sense of determination, he dug into his burger. He needed to have a conversation with Liam about their next steps. And for that, they needed a motel room with electricity to charge and activate their new phones.

Feeling better with food in his belly, Garrett carried Micah back to the SUV with Liz walking beside him. Anyone looking in their direction would assume they were a family. And he found himself liking that image, more than he should.

Knowing now about Liz's loss and her dedication to serving low-income women, he doubted she was looking for anything like a relationship. Especially living as far away as she did.

Enough... There was no point in going down that road, even in his unspoken thoughts. He drove past all the motels, which were surprisingly located in a cluster—maybe because of the prison—and chose the one most likely to accept cash.

"Wait here, okay?" He pushed out of the car and strode inside. All three of the motels appeared fairly busy— probably due to the season—but thankfully, he was able to obtain two connecting rooms for cash.

Micah was awake and looking around when they entered their adjoining rooms. For a minute, Garrett simply gazed down at the curious baby, who looked up at him with dark eyes.

Rebecca had brown eyes, but he'd heard from Liam and Shauna that a baby's eye color could change in the first few months. It didn't matter to him one way or the other; he liked the idea of Micah sharing some of Rebecca's traits.

He wished again that she'd called him about the danger. When Micah's eyelids finally drifted shut, he went about charging and activating the phones.

When they were finally ready, he handed one to Liz, then used the other to call the Green Lake County Sheriff's Department.

"This is Deputy Nichols," he said when the dispatcher answered. "Is Liam around?"

"He's out on patrol but told me to patch you through if you called. Please hold."

Garrett winced at the thought of Liam being forced out on patrol, likely due to his absence. And the fact that he'd asked Wyatt and Abby to help him late into the night. But the situation couldn't be helped. It was better for everyone if he kept the gunmen out of Green Lake.

No matter how much he wished he had his fellow deputies here to back him up.

"Garrett?" Liam's voice broke into his thoughts. "What in the world is going on?"

"I guess you heard from the Volver County Sheriff's Department."

"They asked me to vouch for you, which of course I did. But they mentioned you shot a man and wounded another. Are you okay? How is Micah?"

Garrett hastened to reassure him. "We're fine. I didn't have a choice, Liam. Micah's crying startled the perp into shooting. I had to stop him."

"I trust your judgment." Liam's support meant the world to him. "I just wish you were closer so we could help."

"It's better for you, Shauna and Ciara if I stay away. What I do need, though, is information. I've been doing some searching online and have a short list of suspects that I could use some help with." He gave Liam the names of Edward, Elaine, Jeremy, Connie and Anita. "These are the possible heirs to the Woodward fortune, now that Rebecca is gone and once Robert succumbs to his cancer. I know you're busy, but when you or the others have time, see if you can find anything more about them."

"I still have that contact within the Chicago PD, too. I'll try him. Is this the number I can reach you at?"

"Yes. Thanks, Liam. I owe you for this."

"Stay tuned. Gotta go." Liam quickly disconnected. But it was only a minute later that his phone rang again. "Liam?"

"No, this is Aaron, the dispatcher. I have a call here from Deputy Jorge Rivera of the Volver County Sheriff's Department."

"Great, put him through." Garrett's pulse spiked. "Deputy Rivera? Do you have something for me?"

"Do you know a Tyler Richardson?" Rivera asked.

"No. Who is he?"

"The dead guy. His prints popped up in the system, as he has a long criminal record. Small time stuff, not attempted murder."

Tyler Richardson. Garrett jotted the name down on a small pad of paper on the desk. If they could connect Tyler Richardson to one of the Woodward heirs, they'd be one step closer to ending this nightmare.

NINE

Leaning forward, Liz read the name Garrett had written down. Tyler Richardson? She'd never heard of the guy, but she quickly understood this was the man he'd been forced to shoot when they were hiding behind the woodpile.

"Are you okay to watch Micah for a bit?" Garrett asked. "I'd like to dig into this guy's background, see if I can connect him to anyone within the Woodward family."

"Of course." She dropped her gaze to the baby sleeping in his carrier. Despite knowing this was a temporary arrangement, she'd fallen hard for this little boy.

He was a fighter, much like his mommy and daddy.

"Lizbeth." Hearing Garrett use her full name in his low, husky voice sent shivers of awareness through her. "You have a beautiful name."

"Thank you." Was that her squeaky voice? She managed a smile. "When I was young, I wished for a Native American–sounding name. But my mother didn't want anything to do with her heritage. Maybe she'd been discriminated against at some point. I know she loved my father." Her expression turned somber. "They died in a motorcycle crash near Green Bay."

"I'm sorry to hear that." He put his arm around her shoulder in a friendly hug. His earthy scent messed with her

mind, and she had to remind herself again that this togeth-
erness was temporary. "I lost my mom when I was young
and was raised by my dad and grandparents. My dad and
grandfather were all about hunting and fishing but tended
to avoid emotional conversations."

"I wondered why you were so good at moving silently
through the woods." She smiled teasingly. "You are much
better than I am."

"Years of practice." He grinned, then stood. "I need to get
searching on our dead guy. He must be connected in some
way to the Woodward family."

She nodded, then drew the diaper bag toward her to get it
organized with the new items she'd purchased at the store: a
larger pack of diapers and wipes, along with more formula
to replace the open cans that hadn't been refrigerated. She
hated to waste them but refused to risk Micah getting sick.

When she'd finished, the baby began to cry. She changed
him, then prepared a bottle. Garrett glanced over. "Do you
want me to feed him?"

"I can do it." She nodded toward the laptop computer.
"Have you found anything?"

"No, other than he's from the Chicago area. Did a short
stint in jail for assault and robbery. I have to admit, he doesn't
seem like the type to go from that to murder for hire."

Murder for hire. The words alone made her shiver. "Will
Liam and your deputies investigate him, too?"

"I hope so. I texted Liam the guy's name and date of
birth." He sighed, turning back to the screen. "Every time
I put the Woodward name into the search engine, more articles pop up. It seems as if the business sector loves to fea-
ture articles on real estate moguls like Robert Woodward."

She crossed over to sit close beside him. When Micah
needed to burp, she lifted him to her shoulder and rubbed

his back. "Have you read any articles about Rebecca's death?"

"Not a single one." He grimaced. "And I would have expected it to be the highest-ranking post. It's obvious the gunmen who took her body are hiding the truth about her death until they've eliminated Micah as a threat."

She nodded slowly. That made sense. If a billionaire CEO had died of a gunshot wound, the news would make headlines across the country, not just here in the Midwest. "Maybe we should fake Micah's death."

Garrett spun around to face her. "That's an interesting idea. But we'd need documentation, wouldn't we?"

"Yes." She held his gaze. "It also means giving up Micah's inheritance."

He waved an impatient hand. "I don't care about that. That much money is the root of all evil. Too many people are desperate and greedy. It's not worth it. Besides, I have no interest in running a huge company like that."

She tipped her head, regarding him thoughtfully. She'd known from the beginning he was an honorable man, but he proved it again and again the more time they spent time together. "You're one of the few people who would look at it that way."

"I'd do anything to get the target off my son's back." His blue eyes were resolute.

"I have death certificates in my clinic, so we could head back to fill one out and file it with the state. We could use a different name for him but list Rebecca Woodward as the mother." She hesitated, then added, "Then I'd need to create another birth certificate for him since I dropped the initial paperwork into the mailbox outside the police station. One that doesn't list Rebecca's name at all." On one hand, she didn't like to lie about something like this—yet, like Garrett, she was determined to do whatever was necessary to keep this little boy from being murdered.

"How do you feel about that?" She was touched by how he held her gaze. "I don't want to get you in trouble, Liz. And we'd be filing false paperwork, which is a crime."

"Yes, it's a crime." She forced a reassuring smile. "But if we don't figure out who is behind these murder attempts soon, I don't see that we have much choice."

He considered her offer, his expression serious. "I've asked so much of you already. I hate putting you in such a difficult position. Wouldn't doing that jeopardize your license?"

It would, so she looked away, hoping he wouldn't notice her hesitation. "I'm willing to do that to keep Micah safe. A baby doesn't deserve to be hunted and killed."

He sighed. "Let's give it a little more time. We have the name of the dead guy, which is more than we've had before."

"That's fine, if you want to wait." She frowned. "For all we know, there's still a gunman staked out at my clinic, waiting for us to show up."

"I'm sure there is. If we go back, you and Micah will have to stay somewhere else while I go in for the documentation."

Faking Micah's death had been her idea, but she didn't like this idea of returning to her clinic. Would the place ever be safe? Even after the person responsible for the murder scheme was put in prison?

For the first time since Willow's death, she wasn't eager to return to her clinic. Never had she been so tempted to walk away. Yet doing so was out of the question. She wouldn't leave her patients in limbo without a safety net.

She'd do her best for her patients up until the moment she lost her nursing license. The thought of never practicing as a midwife was difficult to bear.

Still, this wasn't the time to ruminate over her future.

Not when danger still dogged them. Garret had taken precautions, but that didn't mean they couldn't be found.

She cuddled Micah close, then reluctantly rose to place him back in his baby carrier.

"I've looked at all of Tyler Richardson's known associates, but there's nothing to link him to the Woodward family." He stared morosely at the computer screen, then abruptly straightened. "Wait a minute—what if one of the family members has spent time in jail?"

"Why would they?" She returned to sit beside him, close to the computer. "There's no reason to commit a crime if they're already rich."

"Not rich enough, if they've hired someone to kill Micah." He typed on the keyboard. "And I'm thinking more along the lines of drug or alcohol abuse."

"Start with the younger ones," she suggested. "They're more likely to have gotten in trouble with the law."

"You'd be surprised," he muttered, but he keyed in the name *Jeremy Woodward*. "One citation for driving under the influence, but no jail time, as it was a first offense."

"Who's his lawyer?"

He shot her a look of admiration. "Good idea. His lawyer is Jacob MacDonald of MacDonald & Associates." He reached over to add that name to the notepad. "Let me check the other family members."

They were on a roll. She had a good feeling that Garrett's investigative skills would provide them a clue. "Looks like Elaine was caught with a small bag of marijuana during a routine traffic stop, but she didn't do jail time, either. Her lawyer was also Jacob MacDonald."

"I'm sensing a theme," she murmured.

"No kidding," he said in a dry tone. He continued working for several minutes, then sat back in the chair. "Nothing on Connie or Anita, though. Edward came up clean, too, although there was one reckless-driving ticket on his record from almost ten years ago. That could have been an OWI—Operating While Intoxicated—that was pled down."

"Maybe Edward's side of the family is responsible for hiring the gunmen. At the very least, Elaine must have gotten her drugs from someone."

"Yeah, but Richardson wasn't busted for having drugs, so there's no way to know if they ever connected. And all of this isn't proof of murder for hire." His earlier excitement seemed to fade. "I hate to say it, but falsifying documents may be the only way out of this mess."

She leaned over to rest her hand on his knee. "Don't give up hope."

He covered her hand with his. His gaze went from her eyes to her mouth, and when he leaned forward, she did the same, meeting him halfway.

His kiss was tentative at first, then grew deeper as he tugged her close. Their positions were awkward, but she didn't care. Reveling in his kiss, the poignant moment was interrupted by the ringing of his disposable cell phone.

Garrett pulled back, fumbling for the device. The bit of confusion on his face made her wonder if he was already regretting their brief kiss.

Because she didn't regret their embrace one bit.

"Liam? Hang on, I'm going to put this on speaker so Liz can hear, too." He hoped his clumsy actions weren't too noticeable as he fought to recover from the emotional and physical impact of Liz's kiss. "Ah, okay. What's up?"

"I received an interesting call about a missing woman by the name of Rebecca Woodward," Liam said, getting straight to the point. "Apparently, she didn't show up for work today, and her family is worried."

"They were forced into reporting her missing since others were aware of her absence," he mused.

"That's what I'm thinking. This guy who called it in mentioned that she may have been traveling and ended up at a local hospital, as she was pregnant and relatively close to her due date. He's calling all police jurisdictions to put us on notice."

"Isn't that kind of him." Garrett knew better than to assume someone was guilty without proof, but he felt certain this guy was involved. "Did he give you a name?"

"Joel Abernathy. Have you heard of him?"

He glanced at Liz as the name clicked. "Yeah, in fact, I have. Rebecca mentioned he was the company's new CFO. It's possible they were dating."

"Interesting. I'm still waiting to hear back from my Chicago PD contact," Liam said. "I'm hoping he has more information on the Woodward family in general."

"That would be nice. I'd like to talk to Joel myself. He may know why she was in danger. Oh, and I discovered both Elaine and Jeremy Woodward were arrested for misdemeanor offenses related to an OWI and marijuana possession. They didn't do any jail time."

"They got the weed from someone," Liam said, echoing Liz's thought. "But low-level drug dealers are a dime a dozen."

"True. Connie and her daughter, Anita, are clean." He thought again about the lawyer for both kids. "I'm going to reach out to the law offices of MacDonald & Associates. If I hint at having information on Rebecca, I might get through."

"Can't hurt to try." Liam was silent for a moment, then

said, "I'll text you Joel's contact information. I also think you should head back to Green Lake. We can protect you easier if you're close."

"We'd only bring trouble your way," he protested.

"Trouble that we can handle better with more resources at our disposal," Liam said. "We want to be there for you and your son."

"Thanks, I'll take that into consideration. By the way, I may need a different vehicle. The gunman that got away likely has the license plate of this one."

"Okay, let me work with Wyatt and Abby on that. Maybe you can meet up with them somewhere."

"That works. And I appreciate your help." He was grateful for Liam's support. "Anything else?"

"No, I just wanted you to know that Rebecca has been officially listed as a missing person."

But not a deceased one. "Thanks. Give Wyatt my new number and have him call me to set up a vehicle swap."

"Will do. Be careful out there."

Garrett ended the call, then turned to face Liz. "I have a bad feeling Rebecca's body will show up soon. I don't see how they can put a lid on her disappearance forever."

"Maybe we should head back to Green Lake." She bit her lower lip. "I like the idea of having your deputies close by."

"Maybe, but we also need the paperwork from your clinic." A trip he'd rather make with a replacement SUV than with the one they were currently using. "Let's wait until I hear from Wyatt."

"Okay."

He sensed her trepidation. From the way she'd reacted earlier, he knew she was putting her nursing license on the line for him.

For Micah, too.

Yet he wanted to have the death forms handy in case they were forced to go that route—something he'd only do as a last resort.

"Then it's probably best if we head to Liberty after we meet with Wyatt and Abby," she said.

"Yeah, I think so, too." Liam hadn't sent the contact information yet for Joel, so he glanced around their connecting rooms. If he had a choice, he'd rather go to the clinic under the cover of darkness, but without night-vision goggles, he was at the same disadvantage as the gunmen. If there was still someone there watching the place. "It's early enough that we should be able to get there and back without too much trouble. Hopefully, we can spend the night here."

"Are we running low on cash? These rooms can't be cheap."

"Abby stashed extra in the computer bag. Wyatt should be able to bring more." He had more than enough money saved in his bank account to repay the deputy. "It's better we continue spending cash to stay off-grid. Food, shelter and supplies for Micah are bare necessities."

"I agree. If I had any cash back at the clinic for you, I'd happily chip in."

"No need." His gaze dropped to Micah's face. "I'm more than capable of providing for my son."

"It's nice to see you bonding with him." She smiled gently. "He needs you, Garrett. Keep that in mind when you put your life on the line to head back to the clinic."

Her comment brought him up short. Who would raise Micah if something happened to him? The baby wouldn't survive being placed with the Woodward family. "Do you have any forms that I can fill out to make you Micah's guardian if something happens to me?"

"What?" Her eyes rounded in surprise. "No, a lawyer

has to do that. And wouldn't you want Micah to go to your friends?"

"No, I'd want you to raise him." He paused, then added, "If you're willing."

"I—uh, of course. But nothing is going to happen to you, Garrett. Don't take any foolish risks, understand?"

"That's the plan." He didn't intend to get shot, but he needed to have a way to make sure Micah would be raised with love and caring.

A woman like Liz could offer that and more.

Before he could turn back to his computer, his phone rang. He recognized Wyatt's number and quickly answered. "Hey, how are things going?"

"Busy, but it's under control," Wyatt assured him. "I hear you need a new vehicle."

"If you and Abby have time, I do." He quickly explained about the gunman he'd shot and the second guy who'd gotten away.

"We can make time. We're not scheduled until three o'clock. Can you meet us halfway?"

"Yes, we can meet at Montello. That's closer to you. Give me an hour or so, okay?"

"Sure thing. We'll rent a replacement, then meet you at the Montello park."

"Thanks again." He disconnected and rose. "I'll get Micah, if you could grab the diaper bag."

"Of course." Liz gestured to the table. "Are you going to leave the computer behind?"

"No, better not." He took a moment to shut it down and pack it away. "Coming back may not be possible."

"That's what I thought." He didn't like how easily she'd adapted to life on the run, being in danger just for delivering a baby. She took the computer case and the diaper bag. "Let's go."

He swept his gaze over their rooms, noticing how Liz had packed everything neatly in the diaper bag. Then he opened the door and peeked out, glancing around warily.

Seeing nothing alarming, he unlocked the SUV and quickly strode over to place Micah in the back seat. He deftly secured the carrier as Liz stored the bags on the floor in the back.

The trip to Montello took a solid hour, in part because he'd taken small highway roads to avoid a tail. Traffic was nonexistent, which helped. After they'd reached city limits, finding the park in the small town was easy enough.

When he pulled into the lot, two SUVs sat side by side in the far corner, away from other vehicles. Both had been backed in, for easy access out of there. He had to smile at Wyatt's and Abby's defensive tactics.

When he pulled up beside them, Wyatt emerged from behind the wheel. Abby quickly joined them, tossing Garrett the key to the second car.

"Thanks for coming." He genuinely appreciated their support. He handed over his service weapon, knowing Liam had promised it to the Volver County Sheriff's Department. Wyatt dropped it into an evidence bag.

"Brought you a replacement." His deputy handed him another gun. "Abby and I think you should come back to Green Lake, where we can back you up easier."

"I don't want to bring danger your way." He slid the gun in his holster, glad it was the same make and model as his own. Then he opened the back passenger door to remove Micah's carrier.

"He's adorable." Abby's smile faded as she glanced at him and Liz, then added, "Seriously, boss, you need to return to the Green Lake area. You know there's a few places you can use to hide out for a while."

The hopeful expression on Liz's face made him feel guilty. Being safe didn't seem like much to ask, yet he hadn't been able to deliver on his promise. "You're right, but there's something we need to do first."

Wyatt held his gaze, then nodded. "Just know we're here to help."

Movement caught his eye, and he turned in time to see a black SUV with tinted windows coming down the street toward the park.

"The gunman! Get the license plate!" He grabbed Liz and pulled her over to the SUV Abby had brought for them.

"I'll go." Wyatt jumped into the SUV he'd driven and peeled out of the parking spot, heading directly toward the approaching vehicle. The black SUV with tinted windows sped up, moving dangerously fast as they tried to escape.

"Get out of here, boss. I'll follow Wyatt." Abby jumped behind the wheel of the car he and Liz had come in. Thankfully, Wyatt was hot on the trail of the tinted-window SUV.

"Let's go." Garrett wished he could join the pursuit, but engaging in a high-speed car chase with Micah in the back seat didn't seem smart.

Yet as he left the park, heading in the opposite direction that Wyatt and the black SUV had taken, he couldn't help wondering how they'd been found.

The gunmen kept showing up, no matter what attempts they made to stay under the radar.

And he was very afraid they wouldn't be able to escape so easily the next time.

TEN

How was it possible the black SUV with tinted windows had shown up in Montello? A wave of desolation hit hard. What did they have to do to shake off these gunmen?

"Did they follow Abby and Wyatt?" The question popped out of her mouth before she could consider how it might sound.

"Maybe." Garrett's expression was hard as stone. "They are seasoned cops who would have watched for a tail, but it could be that the gunman managed to stay far enough back to escape their notice."

"You think these guys just assumed Wyatt and Abby were coming to meet with us?" She couldn't wrap her mind around it.

He shrugged, his gaze bouncing between the highway ahead and the rearview mirror. "Either that or they tracked our license plate."

"How? It's not like we have toll booths or anything."

"I don't know." His voice was low, and she realized he was beating himself up over this. The situation was hardly his fault.

"I'm sorry. I'm not blaming you." She put a hand on his arm. "It's just frustrating."

"For me, too."

More so for him, as his son was the true target. Despite the all-too-real possibility of losing her nursing license, forging death paperwork for Micah was looking like the best option.

Though she couldn't help wondering if it would work. It made sense that Micah not being an heir would mitigate the danger. Yet these guys seemed incredibly ruthless. So much so, that even with that paperwork filed with the state, they'd still seek to eliminate the possibility of Micah ever claiming his birthright.

When she noticed they were heading northeast, she voiced her concern. "Getting the forms from the clinic doesn't guarantee this will be over. We need to be prepared that simply filing Micah's death notice may not eliminate the threat."

"I know. I've considered that, too." He sighed. "I only intend to do that as a last resort."

"Okay, how long until we reach Liberty?" She wasn't as familiar with the state highways as he seemed to be. "I assume that's our destination."

"It is, and it's almost two hours from here. I'm hoping Wyatt and Abby will have information for us on the black SUV soon."

She nodded, a wave of exhaustion hitting hard. Her emotions were all over the place, making it difficult to concentrate. "I'm sure someone is keeping an eye on the clinic."

"Trust me, I'm taking that into consideration. My plan is to go in on foot. You'll take over behind the wheel, staying on the road with Micah. I'd like you to keep driving until I call with a location to be picked up."

She glanced back at the sleeping infant with trepidation. Being alone with him was a big responsibility. She wasn't armed and was limited as to what she could do to protect him. Yet she couldn't come up with an alternative solution, either. "Okay."

He must have sensed the reservation in her tone. "I'll program Wyatt's and Abby's numbers in your phone. You can call them if you need help."

"Sounds good." Green Lake was an hour from Liberty, but she assumed they'd meet her halfway. If the gunmen didn't shoot out her tires, the way they had with Rebecca's caddy, she should be able to make it.

Best not to focus on the worst-case scenario. That was only asking for trouble. She'd pray for God's protection for Micah and Garrett. His role in this mission was far more dangerous.

"I keep the birth notices and the death notices in the bottom desk drawer on the right." She grimaced. "I haven't had time to submit the birth notice for Micah yet, which will work in our favor."

"I know." His expression remained grim. "I also understand that your career is at stake here."

"It will all work out." She forced all the confidence she could muster into her tone. "Micah's safety trumps everything."

He nodded but didn't say anything more. The rental SUV ate up the highway until she finally saw a sign that indicated Liberty was five miles ahead.

Being even this close to her clinic, the scene of Rebecca's death and the gunmen who'd shot at them made her shiver. She wasn't surprised when Garrett pulled off the highway just under three miles from their destination.

After he'd programed her phone with Wyatt's and Abby's numbers, and that of the dispatcher for Green Lake, he pushed open his door. "Keep your phone handy. I'll let you know when I'm clear."

"I'll be waiting." She slid out of her seat and walked around to the driver's side. Then she wrapped her arms around his waist and hugged him tight.

"Hey, don't worry." His low voice vibrated near her ear. "I'll be okay. Just keep far away from here for a while, okay?"

She nodded and forced herself to release him. "Be careful, Garrett. Micah needs you."

I *need you.*

She swallowed the words before they could tumble from her lips. How ridiculous, to be thinking about her needs when they were still in danger.

She climbed up behind the wheel and closed the door. Garrett flashed a quick smile before he headed into the woods. In a matter of seconds, he disappeared from view.

Shifting the gear into Drive, she pulled away from the edge of the road. After executing a Y turn, she headed back in the direction from where they'd come.

Realistically, it would take Garrett at least thirty minutes to make the trip to her clinic. Maybe longer. And that same amount of time to return. In the meantime, she needed to stay far away from the area.

As she drove south, she whispered a silent prayer: *Lord Jesus, keep Garrett safe in Your care!*

Garrett melted into the woods, listening to the sounds around him. As he moved deeper into the dense forest, he searched for signs that the gunmen were hiding out there.

After covering a mile and a quarter, he caught the first sign likely left by the gunmen: a cigarette butt. He didn't have evidence bags, but he carefully picked up the remnant and dropped it into his pocket. If they made it back to Green Lake without incident, he'd ask Liam to check for prints and, more importantly, DNA.

Slowing his pace, he continued forward, making a large circle around the clinic. If anyone was hiding out here, he wanted to be able to sneak up behind them.

The trip through the woods took longer than he'd anticipated, but his patience was rewarded when he found another cigarette butt. This one still reeked of smoke, making him think it was fresh. He dropped that in his pocket, too, in case there was more than one gunman out here who smoked.

He was surprised the perp wasn't professional enough to have fieldstripped his cigarette butt—or better yet, refrained from smoking at all. Maybe this guy was lower on the totem pole, trusted only to keep watch on a location to which they were not likely to return.

If not for needing the forms, he wouldn't be here at all. He changed his route to get closer to the clinic. When he caught sight of movement about twenty yards ahead, he froze.

The gunman keeping watch moved restlessly from one foot to the other. The guy didn't have his weapon in hand, but a lethal-looking pistol was tucked in a belt holster.

With minute slowness, Garrett lowered to a crouch, watching and waiting. The gunman up ahead kept his gaze forward rather than scanning his surroundings.

A rookie mistake. One he'd use to his advantage.

Having a gunman in custody would help them uncover who was behind these relentless attacks. Granted, he suspected this guy wouldn't know much, but anything was better than what they currently had.

After a few minutes, it was clear this guy was bored. When he lit a cigarette, Garrett eased closer. The smoking gunman must have sensed someone coming up behind him, because he finally turned to look over his shoulder.

Garrett lunged forward, tackling the smoker to the ground. Thankfully, the lit cigarette flew from his fingers. The gunman tried to grab for his gun, but it was too late. Garrett wrenched the weapon free and tossed it into the brush behind him.

Holding the guy firmly on the ground, his hand over his mouth, he whispered, "How many others?"

The guy's eyes widened, then narrowed as if he recognized him as the target he was supposed to be looking for. Garrett suspected he wasn't going to cooperate, but he tried again.

"How many? If you don't want to talk, I'll shoot you and figure it out for myself." He was bluffing, as he would never shoot a man in cold blood, but this guy didn't know that.

The gunman made an attempt to talk, so Garrett loosened his grip. "One. On the other side."

He could be lying, but there was no mistaking the fear in his eyes. Garrett quickly shifted his weight so he could grab the guy's wrists. The perp began to struggle, but again, a second too late. He had a zip tie out and wrapped around his wrists before the guy could escape. Then he quickly patted him down, finding a knife in his pocket.

"Let me go!"

"Quiet." Garrett tugged him up into a sitting position, then used the perp's knife to cut a strip of cloth from the bottom of his shirt to gag him. When that had been accomplished, he zip-tied his ankles to keep him in place. "Behave, and I'll be back. Give me trouble, and I can easily leave you here to rot."

The guy watched him warily, as if ready to believe Garrett was capable of that and worse. Good. He needed this guy to be afraid of him.

Moving faster now, he made it to Liz's clinic without seeing anyone else. But that didn't mean someone else wasn't out there. Finding the forms was the easy part. He used duct tape to keep the envelope containing the documents adhered to his chest. Then he left the clinic as quickly as he'd entered.

He wasn't out of danger yet. He swiftly covered the distance to where he'd left the gunman. Trussed like a turkey, the perp glared at him. Interesting that his cry to be let go hadn't brought the other guy over.

Unless there wasn't another gunman hanging around nearby.

Garrett knelt beside him. "Where's your buddy?" he whispered.

The guy shrugged and looked away.

Hesitating, Garrett considered his options: head out to look for a possibly nonexistent perp or simply leave the area, dragging this guy with him. The problem with the second option was that he didn't believe the smoker was capable of moving quietly. If there was another bad guy lurking close, he'd likely hear them from a mile away.

Then again, why wasn't the second guy here already?

He slit the zip ties around the guy's ankles, then drew him upright. They'd barely gone ten yards when he heard a twig snap.

Garrett hit the ground, pulling the perp with him. Gunfire rang out but didn't come close to hitting them. He shoved the perp behind one tree, then took cover behind another.

Movement through the trees indicated there was someone out there heading toward them. Apparently, the guy had been honest about the presence of a second perp.

Hopefully, there weren't more.

Garrett remained still, making the second gunman come to him. He hoped the bound perp wouldn't try to make a run for it. If he was smart, he'd stay put because the other gunman was likely to shoot the first thing that moved.

Unfortunately, the bound man didn't have the brains to figure that out for himself. He abruptly stood and began to run.

More gunfire rang out, this time pinpointing the shooter's location. Garrett returned fire as the bound guy fell face-first into the ground.

Had he been shot? Garrett's pulse spiked with horror, but he kept his gaze trained for more gunfire. Unfortunately, the shooter remained well hidden, too.

Garrett wanted to believe he'd wounded him, but without hard evidence, he couldn't assume the threat had been disabled. Ignoring the urge to check on the bound man who'd foolishly tried to run, he eased from one tree trunk to the next, carefully edging toward the spot where he'd last glimpsed the shooter.

It took an incredibly long time for him to cover the distance. When he was finally close enough to see a man's body lying in a crumpled heap on the ground, he still didn't lower his guard.

Using another tree trunk for cover, he inched forward until he could see the blood on the man's dark shirt. Carefully, he leaned down to check for a pulse.

Nothing. The shooter was dead.

Frustrated, he rifled through his pockets, not surprised to find a disposable phone and cash. Then he turned to quickly make his way back to check the other assailant. What if he lost both these men? They'd have no hope in figuring out who'd hired them.

When he came closer, though, he heard the bound perp whimpering behind his gag. He was still alive! Garrett pulled him upright and quickly looked for evidence of an injury. Other than the scratches and soreness that had come from his wild dash through the woods, he was unharmed.

"You shouldn't have tried to run." He pushed him against the tree, then searched for the other guy's gun. He saw it lying nearby and stuck it in the back of his waistband for evidence.

Garrett took another minute to text Liz, letting her know he was fine and that he was on his way back to the highway. Almost seventy minutes had passed since she'd dropped him off, and they still had a lot of ground to cover.

Her response was almost immediate, saying she was ready to meet him anytime. Grateful to know she was okay, he turned his attention to the bound man.

"Let's go." He nudged him forward, refusing to remove the zip ties from his wrists or the stretch of cloth over his mouth. Another gunman might be hiding nearby.

Their trek through the woods was hardly as quiet as he would have liked. He tried to remain hidden in the trees, moving without drawing too much attention. It bothered him that the bound man stumbled often, brushing against branches and generally making more noise than an entire herd of deer.

Despite the possible danger from others, he didn't follow the same circular path he had to get here. Time was of the essence.

He wanted—*needed*—to get back to Liz and Micah.

After a mile, he took a break. The bound man seemed out of shape, as he leaned weakly against a tree. Maybe his stumbling around wasn't an act. It was the first crack in the armor of these hired hit men, and he needed to bust it open to his advantage.

But not until they were safely away from Liz's clinic. He waited another mile before texting Liz again.

Meet us at mile marker 23.

Again, her response was swift. Us?

Long story. Be there in 15 to 20.

I'll be waiting.

Liz's last message sent a wave of warmth through him. He knew better than to make a big deal out of their brief but poignant kiss. It was natural for them to become close while they were on the run and in danger. It didn't mean anything.

Still, it had been a long time since anyone had waited for him to come home.

He ruthlessly pushed the bound perp to go faster, letting him know they were almost at their destination. The guy was sweating profusely by the time they arrived at the mile marker.

Liz was parked along the side of the highway, the SUV as welcoming as anything he'd ever seen. She jumped out of the car when he emerged from the woods with his prisoner.

"Are you alright?" She raked her gaze over him, then glanced curiously at the perp. "Who's this?"

"Not sure. He was stationed in the woods, watching the front of your clinic." He removed the gag from the gunman's mouth, then opened the front passenger door. "Get in. Liz, you should sit in back with Micah." Even though the perp didn't have a weapon, he wasn't about to trust him to be near his son.

"I'm glad you're back." A frown furrowed her brow. "You didn't get the forms."

"I did." He gestured for her to climb in. "I'll explain later. We need to get out of here."

She looked confused but nodded and took the seat beside Micah's carrier. Then he slid in behind the wheel. "What's your name?" he asked as he pulled away from the highway marker.

"Lawyer."

"That's fine. You can lawyer up. After all, you have the right to remain silent. Anything you say can and will be used against you in a court of law. And you already know you have the right to an attorney. If you can't afford one, you will be appointed one at no cost to you." Garrett tried to sound casual as he recited the perp's Miranda rights, when he really wanted to shake the truth out of him. "But I don't know why you'd take the rap for attempted murder when it was someone else who hired you to do his dirty work. He'll hire a replacement for you quicker than you can blink."

The guy didn't respond; he turned to look out the window.

Garrett ground his teeth together in frustration but managed to remain calm. "Liz, call Deputy Wyatt Kane. Let him know we have a gunman in custody. They'll put him into the system, and we'll find out who he's associated with soon enough. His financial records will likely tell the tale."

"Happy to." She made the call while the perp beside him shifted nervously in his seat.

"Could you really kill a baby?" He cast a sideways glance at the guy. "Just because someone told you to?"

"I didn't kill anybody," the perp muttered.

"You tried to kill me. We found shell casings that will likely match the gun I took from you." Garrett smiled without humor. "Attempted murder of a cop holds a higher sentence."

For a long moment, there was nothing but silence. Then

the guy blurted out, "I was hired by a guy named Joel Abernathy."

Joel Abernathy? Seriously? He caught Liz's gaze in the rearview mirror. She went to work on her phone, texting Wyatt.

A few minutes later, she gasped. "You were right, Garrett. Joel Abernathy is Rebecca's fiancé."

"What? Are you sure?" He felt as if he'd been kicked in the chest. Dating was one thing, but engaged to be married? While she was pregnant?

She lifted the phone. "According to Wyatt, they found an article announcing their engagement."

Stunned speechless, his mind reeled. Rebecca had never intended to tell him about his son.

She'd promised to marry a man who would have become Micah's father. A man who may have gone as far as hiring someone to kill his son!

ELEVEN

Liz thought back to those tense moments when Rebecca had arrived at her clinic in full-blown labor. The woman had never mentioned a man named Joel, much less that he was her fiancé. Liz's focus had been on delivering the baby and trying to save Rebecca's life. She'd remembered seeing her carefully manicured hands—but had Rebecca worn an engagement ring?

Yes, now that she thought about it, she *had* seen a large diamond ring.

"Why does Joel Abernathy want Micah dead?" Garrett's question interrupted her thoughts. "What difference does it make to him if there's a baby in the picture?"

The bound man hunched his shoulders. "Abernathy didn't ask me to kill the kid. He wanted the kid brought to him."

That was interesting news. "Then why keep shooting at us when the baby was nearby?" she asked. "You could have killed him."

"I didn't try to kill the baby," the guy repeated. "And I'm not saying anything more until I talk to my lawyer."

"That's your right," Garrett said. "Just keep in mind we want the man behind these attempts. And try to remember that some rich people believe they're above the law. A guy like Joel only looks out for himself in these situations."

She was impressed with how Garrett seemed to know just what to say. The bound man remained silent, but she could tell he was considering Garrett's words. She felt certain this guy would eventually tell them what he knew once he'd lawyered up and could arrange to exchange information for a lighter sentence.

A text came through on her phone. "Wyatt is asking that we meet in Oshkosh."

"That works." Garrett met her eyes in the rearview mirror. "How is Micah?"

"He's sleeping." She texted Wyatt back, then glanced at her watch. Even though how they'd been on the run from one location to the next, Micah seemed to be on a regular schedule. Unusual for newborns, but something she was grateful for in this case. He'd likely wake up soon, needing to be fed. Thank goodness they'd purchased more canned formula for him.

When Garrett nodded and lapsed into a brooding silence, she wondered what was going through his mind. The news of Rebecca's engagement had seemed to rattle him. Not that she blamed him for being stunned.

Both Wisconsin and Illinois state laws deemed any baby born to a married couple provides parental rights to both spouses, regardless of who might be the real biological father. Was Joel's intent to get his hands on the baby so he could have access to the Woodward fortune? Wasn't it too late for that? He and Rebecca weren't married. And while he might claim the baby was his, a simple DNA test would prove otherwise.

If they had gotten married, pictures would be plastered all over social media and picked up by newspapers. Right?

She texted Wyatt. Did Joel and Rebecca get married?

It took several long moments before she received an answer. Abby says no record of a marriage between them has been found on file.

Thanks.

"Let Wyatt know we're fifteen minutes from Oshkosh. I need to know exactly where he wants to meet."

She relayed the information. Wyatt responded, asking to meet at a popular restaurant located just off the interstate. The thought of food made her stomach growl, but they would hardly be able to enjoy a meal having the bound guy along as their passenger.

Micah began to squirm five minutes later. She wanted to take him out of his car seat, but she hesitated since they were still on the interstate. She quickly made a bottle, then gave it to him while he was still in the car seat. She cuddled as close as she could to provide skin-to-skin contact by pressing the top of his head into the curve of her neck. She worried he was spending too much time in the baby carrier and not enough being held and loved.

If only they could find a safe location to stay for a while. Not that she wasn't grateful for the protection they'd had so far. She firmly believed God was watching over them during this difficult time.

"Is he okay?" Garrett asked.

"Great." She forced a smile. "Babies are resilient."

Garrett's gaze clung to hers for a moment before his eyes shifted to examine the road ahead. She wanted to ask him what he was thinking but knew he didn't want to talk in front of their prisoner.

They arrived at their destination just as Micah finished his bottle. She quickly removed him from the car seat, then held him up to her shoulder so he could burp. She nuzzled the downy, dark hair on his head.

She prayed Joel Abernathy wouldn't get anywhere near this little baby. Not when she suspected he only wanted the infant for his own personal gain.

Unless he really did believe the baby was his. The thought brought her gaze to Garrett, but he was already pushing out of the car and going around to open their prisoner's door.

The more the idea circled around in her mind, the more she believed Joel may not be as much of a bad guy as they'd originally thought.

She opened her car door to hear better, but she stayed where she was, holding Micah close while Wyatt and Abby joined Garrett and the prisoner.

"I instructed him on his rights, and he says he wants a lawyer," Garrett explained. "He mentioned being hired by Joel Abernathy. I'd like to follow you back to Green Lake so we can arrange a meeting with Abernathy. Liam was going to text me his contact info but hasn't. I'd like to talk to him one-on-one if possible."

"If Liam agrees, that's fine with me." Wyatt held the prisoner's arm in a firm grip. "This perp should ride in our vehicle in case you need to take a different route."

"Agreed. What happened with the black SUV?"

Wyatt shook his head, glancing at the prisoner as if he didn't want to say too much. "He escaped, but I sent the license plate to Dispatch. We haven't heard back yet. Things have been busy back there, between a series of robberies and a boating incident on Green Lake."

"That's understandable. By the way, there's a dead man in the woods near Liz's clinic." Garrett gestured to the prisoner. "His backup started shooting, so I was forced to return fire. I would suggest we let the local police know, but it's possible that the dead guy has been picked up by now, the way the others were."

"You've been busy, too," Abby said with a frown. "We'll reach out, mention a report of gunfire in the area. Can't hurt to have someone go check the place out."

"Good. Better that way. I can't afford to turn over my weapon again. Not until this is over." Garrett glanced back at Liz, then gestured to the restaurant. "We haven't eaten in a while. I'd like to grab something here before heading back."

"Fine with us," Abby said. "But we should talk about the proposed interview with Abernathy. We want to be sure to have plenty of backup if you end up arranging a meeting."

"Okay, we can discuss that more later." Garrett smiled wearily. "Thanks for everything. We'll be in touch when we hit city limits."

"Be careful." Wyatt nodded at Liz before leading the prisoner to their SUV. Abby walked along on the other side; then they took a moment to replace the zip ties with actual handcuffs.

Garrett came over to where Liz sat with Micah. He reached for the baby, and she quickly handed him over.

"I'm still in shock over Rebecca's engagement," he confided in a low tone. "But that explains why she didn't tell me she was pregnant."

Her heart ached for him. "It could be that Joel believes the baby is his."

Garrett frowned. "Maybe, but sending gunmen after us to get him back is hardly the way to go."

"True. But he may have assumed we were keeping the baby for other reasons. Especially since he reported Rebecca's disappearance." She shrugged. "Maybe he doesn't deserve the benefit of the doubt, but you're right about the need to hear what he has to say."

"I know." Garrett kissed Micah's head, melting her heart even more. "I guess going back to the clinic ended up working out. We know more information now than we did before."

Those hours spent waiting for him had not been easy. Her mind had conjured up all sorts of scenarios, none of them good. It was only after she'd received his text saying he was okay and would be meeting her that she'd been able to relax.

The idea of something bad happening to Garrett filled her with dread. She cared about him, far more than she should.

And not just because he was protecting her and Micah, too.

He was an honorable guy, one who was finding his way back to his faith. She admired his strength, his courage and his compassion.

Leaving him and Micah behind once this was over would be the second-hardest thing she'd have to do in her entire life.

Losing her daughter was still the most difficult. But leaving Garrett and his son would leave a similar gaping hole in her heart.

Pushing away his own disappointment and shock, Garrett focused on their next steps. He wanted to set up a meeting with Joel as soon as possible, but his stomach was rumbling with hunger, and he was sure Liz's was, too. They hadn't eaten since their early lunch, and it was going on five thirty in the afternoon by now.

Nourishment was important if they were going to get to the bottom of this. No matter what the prisoner claimed, there had been so much gunfire since this started that it was nothing short of amazing that Micah hadn't been hit.

No, he wasn't about to give Abernathy the benefit of the doubt. Not yet.

He caught Liz's gaze. "Are you hungry? We should grab a bite while we're here."

"Yes, that would be great. That way I can change Micah, too."

"I can do it. Would you unbuckle the car seat? And grab the diaper bag?" He couldn't explain his reluctance to set the baby down. Or hand him over to Liz. It wasn't that he didn't trust her—he did. He liked holding his son, feeling his small weight curled on his chest. It wasn't fair that they hadn't had much time to bond.

Hopefully soon, though. Once the danger was over, he would ask for Liz's advice on what he needed to buy, then formally submit the paperwork for his leave of absence from work. Liam had already approved some time off, but he wanted the full paternity leave.

He was looking forward to the days when he could concentrate solely on his son.

"Here you go." Liz handed him the diaper bag, hauling the empty carrier into the restaurant herself. He followed her inside and waited until they were seated in a booth before taking Micah to the restroom to change him.

The way his son gazed up at him filled him with love. How anyone could hire a gunman to take out a baby was beyond belief. And, in his opinion, anyone that heartless should be prosecuted to the fullest extent of the law.

When he returned to the table with Micah, Liz was studying the menu. They had fresh water, which he gladly gulped after he'd slid in across from her.

He kept Micah in the crook of his arm while he looked at the restaurant's offerings. He decided on a French dip sandwich, then pushed the plastic menu aside.

Liz set her menu aside, too, smiling at the sleeping baby. Then her expression turned serious. "It might be better to wait until tomorrow before meeting with Joel."

Before he could respond, their server came to take their order. Once they were alone, he shook his head. "It's time to put an end to this nightmare. It will still be light out by the time we get to Green Lake."

"But not for long," she protested. "You don't want to risk being ambushed in the dark."

He would take whatever risk was necessary to get Joel Abernathy in police custody. "We'll see what Liam thinks. Wyatt and Abby are working a second shift. It would be nice to have them as backup."

She grimaced and sighed. "You're right. I trust Abby and Wyatt to have our back."

When their food arrived, he reluctantly placed Micah back in his carrier. The sleeping baby didn't seem to mind, but his arms felt empty without his warm presence.

Liz reached out to take his hand. "Dear Lord, we are grateful for this food You've provided for us. Please continue to keep us all safe in Your care, especially Garrett, as he may face more danger tonight. Amen."

"Amen." He gently squeezed her hand. "I'll be fine. The good news is that this will all be over soon."

"I know." She dug into her roasted chicken while he enjoyed his roast beef. The simple meal helped rejuvenate his flagging energy. He was anxious to get back on the road to Green Lake.

When he pulled out some cash to pay their bill, he realized he'd forgotten to ask Abby and Wyatt to replenish his funds. They weren't going back to their previous motel room and would need to find another place to stay.

As if reading his thoughts, Liz asked, "Do you have enough?"

"Yes, we'll be fine." He could either get more from an ATM or maybe stop at his place. He wouldn't mind a change of clothes. The warm temps were nice in some respects, but he was sweaty after his long trek through the woods to Liz's clinic and back.

Remembering how he'd attached the envelope to his chest, he reached up to remove it, wincing at the amount of hair he pulled off with the tape.

"I wondered where you'd put that." Liz smiled ruefully as she took the envelope from him. "I'm glad you found the documents, but it appears we won't need them, after all."

He shrugged. "It was worth it to get one of the gunmen in custody. I have a feeling Abernathy's operation will come crumbling down once he realizes it's in his best interest to tell us what he knows."

"I agree." She tucked the envelope into the diaper bag. "I'm ready to go when you are."

He took a moment to make sure Micah was strapped in, then stood. He felt certain they hadn't been followed, but he swept his gaze over the area, anyway.

It was a little troublesome that they hadn't learned who the black SUV with tinted windows was registered to. Maybe the vehicle had been stolen or the license plates switched out—two common tactics used by criminals.

Once they were settled in their vehicle, he headed back to the interstate. The black SUV bothered him. There had been no sign of the car used by either the dead man or the guy he'd captured outside Liz's clinic. How many hired gunmen were still out there? At least one: the driver of the black SUV.

Likely more.

"Let me know when you'd like me to text Wyatt and Abby." Liz's voice broke into his thoughts. "You said we'd let them know when we reached city limits."

"Right." He'd almost forgotten that. "I might swing by my place first. I desperately need a change of clothes."

She frowned. "Are you sure it's safe?"

He couldn't be sure of anything, but the way the gunmen had been following him and staking out her clinic indicated they may have someone at his place, too. He considered his options, then said, "We'll use the same approach as the clinic. I'll have you drop me off, then head to our head-quarters. I know my property better than anyone else. I'm sure I can get in and out without being seen."

"Okay." She looked troubled by his decision, but his main concern was her safety—and Micah's, too.

When they were only five miles from Green Lake, he nodded at her. "Let Wyatt and Abby know we're close."

She used her phone to text them, then added, "I don't see why they can't meet us at your place."

It wasn't a bad idea. "You can ask, but they are working, and it's busy with tourists. Don't be upset if they can't take the time."

"I understand." She continued working on the phone, then grinned. "They're on their way to your house."

"Good." Maybe it was for the best. They could use the time to come up with a plan to run past Liam. If the three of them could agree, their boss likely would, too.

The sun was dipping low on the horizon by the time he pulled into his long driveway. He could see a pair of head-lights near his log home and knew Wyatt and Abby had already arrived. Confident they'd have scouted the place for danger, he pulled up alongside them and quickly slid out from behind the wheel.

"The yard is clear," Wyatt informed him.

"Thanks. Why don't you all come inside?" He opened the back passenger door to remove Micah's infant seat. "We can talk after I change my clothes."

Abby shrugged. "Why not?"

Liz joined him as he lifted Micah's carrier and led the way up to his front door. He hesitated, realizing the door wasn't locked, but then remembered that they'd left in a hurry.

"Liz, take the baby. Abby, stand guard. Wyatt and I will clear the house, just to be safe."

Wyatt pulled his weapon. "Let's do it."

He pushed the door open, then stayed to one side, listening intently. A bad smell coming from inside made him wrinkle his nose. What in the world? Had an animal died in there?

Ignoring the stench, he went first, with Wyatt close behind. The moment they passed over the threshold, they spread out in different directions. He took the hallway leading to the bedrooms, where the putrid scent grew worse.

He pushed open the door to his master suite, freezing in place when he spied the source of the awful smell.

Rebecca's missing dead body had been found. She'd been left on his bed, likely in an attempt to implicate him in her murder.

TWELVE

"Get back." Abby's tone was sharp.

"What's wrong?" The abrupt change in the female deputy's demeanor indicated something was amiss.

"I need you and Micah to return to the SUV." Abby gripped her arm and tugged her toward the vehicle.

"Wait." She dug in her heels. Abby hadn't pulled her weapon, so she didn't think there was a gunman nearby. "I want to know what happened."

Abby didn't answer, speaking instead into her radio as she continued pulling her toward the SUV. Reluctantly, Liz complied, for Micah's sake.

"Ten-four." Abby let go of her radio. "Liam will be here soon."

"Why? What did they find inside Garrett's house?" After having been shot at on several occasions, she was irritated they didn't deem it important enough to keep her in the loop.

Abby hesitated, then nodded. "I guess you deserve to know. Rebecca Woodward's body was in Garrett's master suite."

"What?" That was not one of the scenarios that had flitted through her mind.

"I know. It's not good." Abby stood almost directly in front of her, the same way Garrett always had. "Obviously, the bad guys were here at some point."

"You mean, other than the night they fired shots at us." Her mind spun. It was inconceivable to imagine a gunman—likely two—carrying Rebecca from the exam table in her clinic to their vehicle, then again inside Garrett's house. "Do you know how long she's been here?"

"No. Maybe the medical examiner will be able to determine a more detailed timeline."

"Poor Garrett." She could only imagine how horrifying it was for him to see the woman he'd once cared for dead in his bed.

"Yeah, but don't worry. No one will believe he had anything to do with her death."

She frowned and straightened. "Of course not. I was there when she died. I delivered Micah while she was still alive, then did my best to save her life. Garrett was miles away when that happened."

"I know, Liz. You don't have to convince me." Abby managed a grim smile. "But casting suspicion on Garrett was the reason she was left here."

The possibility made her shiver, especially if the gunmen had ended up succeeding in killing her and Garrett. Had Joel Abernathy orchestrated all of this? How far would he go to get Micah back?

Before she could say anything more, sirens wailed in the distance. She glanced over her shoulder, not surprised to see red and blue lights flashing in the darkness.

Garrett and Wyatt quickly joined them. The somber expression on Garrett's features tugged at her heart. Leaving Micah's baby carrier in the car, she closed the gap between them, reaching for his hand.

To her surprise, he pulled her close in a tight hug. She melted against him, offering her support. "I'm so sorry," she whispered.

He pressed a kiss to her temple without saying a word.

She understood how the reality of seeing a loved one dead was worse than just hearing the news.

And it would be ten times worse to see that person stretched out like a victim in your own bed.

A police vehicle pulled up next to the SUV. The sirens had been silenced, but the red and blue lights continued to whirl, casting the area in an eerie glow.

Garrett loosened his embrace, taking a step back. She let him go, wishing there was more she could do for him.

"Thanks for coming, Liam." He gave the sheriff a nod. "We cleared the house while preserving evidence."

"You believe Abernathy is responsible?" Liam asked.

"It's the only thing that makes sense." Garrett gestured to his home. "According to our perp, he was hired by Abernathy to get Micah. Liz pointed out that he may believe the baby is his."

"Are you sure he's not?" Liam asked.

"Rebecca told me Garrett was the father and begged me to get Micah to Garrett so he would be safe," Liz told him. "I hardly think a woman who is dying would lie about something so important."

"Yet she hadn't told Garrett about the baby beforehand, either." Liam's reasonable tone was annoying. "Obviously, a DNA test will confirm which of you is the baby's father."

Garrett cleared his throat. "I understand what you're saying, but the timing works. I was with Rebecca the night after Jason was killed in the line of duty. No excuses, but I was a wreck that night. And Rebecca was there for me."

Liam nodded slowly. "Okay. Crime scene techs are on the way. They'll go over your place with a fine-tooth comb."

She remembered Garrett's plan to change out of his sweaty clothes. "Can Garrett get clean clothes without disturbing anything important?"

"No need. It's fine." Garrett frowned. "I don't want anything out of my room now."

She could certainly understand his reluctance.

"I have some things that should fit," Wyatt offered.

"Thanks." Garrett turned to Liam. "We need to set up a meeting with Abernathy ASAP."

"I'm open to suggestions," Liam agreed. "But first, we need to wait until your home has been processed and Rebecca is safely in the morgue."

"We need to keep her death a secret," Abby said. "If the newshounds realize she was found dead here in Green Lake, they'll descend on us like locusts."

"She's right," Garrett said. "That's a circus we don't need."

Liam grimaced. "Okay, I can keep it quiet for at least twenty-four hours—but sooner or later, the news is going to leak." He scowled. "It always does."

"Yeah, I hear you." Garrett raked a hand over his hair. "Once we draw Abernathy out of hiding, the danger will be over. From there, we can reach out to her father to give them the news before he hears it from the media."

"If he's still able to understand what's going on," Liz felt compelled to point out. She didn't like being the bearer of bad news, but they needed to keep their expectations realistic. "Cancer care isn't my area of expertise, but people generally lose their cognitive ability during the dying process. The brain simply shuts down, and the body soon follows."

There was a long pause as the group digested that information.

"We need to move quickly, then," Liam finally said, breaking the silence. "I'll put in a call to Abernathy myself since he reported Rebecca as a missing person. I'll let him know he needs to come make a positive ID."

"He'll know she's already dead," Wyatt said. "Why would he bother?"

Garrett spoke in a low voice. "Tell him we have her baby. That should convince him to come."

Liz stared at him. "But you're not giving him Micah."

"No, of course not." Garrett met her gaze. "We'll arrest him for attempted murder for hire."

"Yet if he knows we have his hired hand in custody, he'll stay far away," Abby pointed out.

"I'll make the call," Liam repeated. "If he doesn't answer, we'll think of something else."

She could tell by the despair in Garrett's eyes that he was thinking the same thing she was.

Abernathy wasn't stupid enough to walk into a trap.

Then she frowned. "Why would Joel kill Rebecca? Wasn't she his ticket to her fortune?"

Garrett shrugged. "Maybe she'd called it off. I have to assume he figured he was better off without her. All he needed to do was take custody of Rebecca's child, the next heir to Woodward Enterprises."

His logic made sense. And if that was what had happened, she could see why Rebecca may have driven all the way to her clinic to have her baby. Maybe she'd planned to take the baby to Garrett afterward.

Only she'd been hunted down and shot before she delivered her child.

Any hope of this ending soon withered away. Danger still lurked nearby, a killer's crosshairs centered on a small newborn baby.

Feeling sick at knowing that Rebecca had been left for him to find, Garrett tried to come up with an idea to coax Abernathy out of hiding.

He turned to Liam. "Let me call him. Greed understands greed. I'll let Abernathy know he can have Micah for a price."

Liz sucked in a harsh breath as if in protest, but he ignored it.

"I'll tell him I know he hired the gunmen who were outside Liz's clinic. I'll claim I shot both men and that I'm willing to make a deal. Wyatt and Abby, among others, can be hiding nearby to grab him."

Liam scowled, but Abby chimed in. "That could work."

"I like it," Wyatt agreed. "At the very least, Abernathy will try to take Micah by force without paying a dime, but we'll be there to stop him."

"I'll keep Micah safe," Liz said. "Garrett can use the carrier with a blanket stuffed inside as a decoy. In the dark, Abernathy won't realize it's empty."

"Fine. We'll give it a try." Liam glanced over to where more cars were coming in. The crime scene techs had arrived.

Garrett refocused on the plan. "I'll use one of the abandoned cabins." He turned to Wyatt and Abby. "Your father's old house would work."

"That's fine with me," Abby said. "Dad is staying in town, in the apartment over Rachel's former café, so he won't be in danger."

Liam was scrolling through his phone. Then he stopped and rattled off a number. Garrett quickly typed it into his phone as a contact.

"Let's head to our place," Wyatt suggested. "I'll get you a clean shirt and jeans, then you can make the call to Abernathy. We'll set up the meeting for later tonight."

"In the dark?" Liz asked. "Are you sure that's wise?"

"The darkness will hide Wyatt and Abby, too." Garrett

flashed a reassuring smile. "Trust me, this will work. You and Micah can stay at headquarters."

She hesitated, then nodded. "Okay. But promise me that you'll call as soon as you have him. I'll be on eggshells until I hear from you."

"I promise. You'll hear from us the minute we have him in custody or at the point we're convinced he isn't going to show." Garrett couldn't guarantee he'd make the call personally, but between the three of them, someone would contact her.

"What about having a deputy stationed at headquarters with her?" Abby asked. "Late at night, it's not as busy."

He glanced at Liam, who nodded. "I'll watch over them."

"Thanks, boss." He gestured to the SUVs. "Let's hit the road. I want to set this plan in motion ASAP."

Five minutes later, they were back on the road, Garrett following Wyatt's SUV. Their small house wasn't that far from his, although it wasn't nearly as rustic. They'd purchased a fixer-upper that still needed some work.

Abby and Wyatt quickly cleared the area before they all headed inside. Wyatt disappeared down the hallway, then returned with a clean black T-shirt and black jeans. He tossed the garments at Garrett.

"Thanks." He used the bathroom to change and then came back to the main room. Pulling out his phone, he glanced at Wyatt. "Should I set this up for midnight?"

"Yeah, that works." Wyatt grinned. "Maybe he'll try to move the time frame up."

"You should hurry," Liz said. "Micah is squirming around. He may need to be changed."

"Hearing a baby crying in the background could work in our favor." When Micah began to whimper, Garrett made the call. As expected, Abernathy didn't pick up, but he left a message with Micah's crying as a backdrop: "Abernathy, I have the kid. I know you hired those goons to grab him. I'm willing to trade him for cash. Call me at this number when you're ready to make a deal."

Liz picked up Micah and carried him over to the sofa with the diaper bag. She crooned to the baby as she changed him. Watching her made his chest ache with longing.

"Do you think he'll call back?" Wyatt asked.

He tore his gaze from Liz. "I hope so."

"He may have more gunmen stationed at the meeting site," Abby said. She fiddled with her phone, then turned the screen toward him. "This is Abernathy and Rebecca's engagement photo."

The sight of Rebecca and Joel together didn't bother him anymore. He made a mental note of the guy's facial features, though. "We'll be prepared. You and Wyatt know that area better than they do. And I'm expecting him to bring backup. The most important thing is to make sure Liz and Micah are safe."

"Agreed," Wyatt said. "We'll be in place before they are."

"I trust you both." He was humbled by their willingness to jump into danger for him—and for his son, of course. "Thanks."

"Hey, we know what it's like, remember?" Wyatt clapped him on the shoulder.

It wasn't that long ago that they'd both been on the run from the Mob. And as awful as that had been, he was grateful he had two great deputies working for him now as a result.

His phone rang, startling him. He almost wished Micah was crying again as he lifted the phone to his ear. "Yeah?"

"How much?" Abernathy's voice was low and hoarse, as if he might be trying to mask it.

"A million." Garrett knew the Woodward fortune was worth a lot more. "I'm not greedy. I only need enough to retire early."

"When?" The guy was not much of a conversationalist.

"Tonight at midnight. I'm sure you can access the cash and transfer the funds electronically. I'll have my computer there and will make sure the cash transfers before you take the kid."

"Fine. Meet me—"

"No, you'll meet me at an old cabin near mile marker 260 off Highway Z. Come alone, or you won't get the kid."

"Midnight." The line went dead.

"Not sure you can really access banking information after hours," Abby said. "I mean, you can access the accounts, but the money won't show up until the next business day."

"Yeah, but he's planning on scamming me out of the money, anyway, just like we're planning to arrest him, so that doesn't matter." He glanced at his watch; it was a quarter past nine o'clock at night. "You and Wyatt need to get out there. I'll drop Liz and Micah off at headquarters, then head over."

"Got it." Wyatt glanced at Abby. "Still wearing your bullet-resistant vest?"

"Yes, but Garrett needs one, too."

When Liz glanced expectantly at him, holding Micah in the crook of her arm, he nodded. "I'll pick one up at the station when I get Liz and Micah inside."

"Sounds like a plan." Wyatt took his wife's hand. "Ready?"

Abby reached up to give him a quick kiss, then turned toward the door. "Let's go."

Garrett escorted Liz and Micah out to the rental. Liz placed Micah in his seat for the ride across town. When they reached headquarters, she put a hand on Garrett's arm, stopping him from getting out of the car.

"You'll be careful, right?"

"Yes. Now more than ever because I have a son to raise." He almost mentioned how much he wanted to see her again, but he held back. He didn't know how she would respond, and going into a dangerous situation with emotional baggage wasn't smart. "One of us will call you as soon as possible."

"I'd rather hear from you." She surprised him by leaning over to kiss his cheek. Then she quickly turned and pushed her door open. He followed suit, taking Micah's baby carrier.

Inside the sheriff's department headquarters, it was quiet. After making sure Liz was settled in his office, he took the empty baby carrier with a blanket stuffed inside and poked his head into Liam's office.

"I'm leaving."

"Be careful." Liam's gaze was solemn. "He's a desperate man."

"I know." He headed back to the car, taking the time to strap in the baby carrier the way he would if Micah was inside.

Finding the abandoned cabin wasn't difficult. He and the other deputies often drove past to make sure kids weren't using it as a party house. There was no sign of Wyatt or Abby when he pulled up the deeply rutted driveway, but he hadn't expected to see them.

Inside the cabin, he set the baby carrier on the wooden kitchen table, then went back for the computer and a flashlight. He opened the laptop and used his phone as a hot spot to get access to the internet. He turned off the flashlight to save the battery, then settled in to wait.

Watching the minutes tick past was agonizing. After a

while, he stood and moved from one window to the other, with only the eerie glow of the computer as light.

He found himself trying to figure out where Abby and Wyatt had stationed themselves. Near enough to respond quickly but far enough to stay out of sight.

They had it harder than he did, crouching in the dark woods surrounding the place.

His phone rang, startling him. There was still an hour until their designated meeting time, but he answered Abernathy's call, anyway.

"Don't try to change the plan," Garrett said in lieu of a greeting. "It's my way or the highway. I can get someone else to pay me for the kid if you don't want to."

"Show me the kid." Abernathy's voice was still hoarse.

Garrett froze, glancing out the windows. Where was he? Did Wyatt and Abby have him in their sights? "I will when you get here."

"I can see you inside with the computer. Lift the brat up and show him to me."

"Hard for me to do that if I don't know where you are." He stalled for time, texting Wyatt on his disposable phone with one hand below the table. "I'm the one calling the shots. You don't want to play the game, I'll get someone else."

Wyatt's response vibrated his disposable phone: Found him. He has only one guy with him. We're moving in.

"Okay, fine," he quickly amended. "Hang on. I have to unbuckle the baby." Vying for time, Garrett tucked the phone between his ear and his shoulder and reached for the baby carrier. He figured Abernathy didn't have binoculars or else he'd already know Micah wasn't here.

He turned his back to the main window, hoping and praying Wyatt and Abby would apprehend them soon.

The sharp retort of gunfire reverberated through the

night. Garrett abandoned the baby carrier and bolted outside, directly toward the spot where he thought Abernathy must be hiding. When he reached the area, though, Abernathy was on the ground, bleeding from a bullet wound.

"Take cover," Wyatt shouted. "Unknown shooters!"

Garrett dove to the side as more gunfire rang out. What in the world was going on? When the gunfire ceased, he belly crawled to the fallen man. Abernathy was still breathing, but blood seeped from a wound high in his upper chest.

It was clear someone else had wanted Abernathy dead, too.

THIRTEEN

Liam stood in the doorway of Garrett's office, his expression grim. "Garrett, Wyatt and Abby are safe and unharmed. But gunfire rang out prior to the planned exchange. Abernathy has been hit."

Liz appreciated that he'd led with the good news. "How bad?"

"He's alive but suffered an upper-chest wound. The ambulance is there now, picking him up. Abby will accompany him to the hospital. Garrett and Wyatt will stay to scour the scene."

The same sort of wound Rebecca had sustained. The difference here was that Abernathy could go straight into surgery without taking time to deliver a baby.

Then the reality of the situation struck hard. "Wait, how did Abernathy get shot? Did Wyatt or Abby hit him by mistake?"

"No, there was an unknown shooter that arrived on the scene." Liam's frown deepened. "Garrett believes Abernathy may have been followed there."

"It doesn't make sense. Who would do that?" As she uttered the words, she knew. "Someone from the Woodward family."

"That's the only thing that makes sense," Liam agreed.

She gazed down at the sleeping baby in her arms. Holding Micah was a joy, even though her arms were getting stiff from being in the same position for so long. A discomfort she gladly ignored. While waiting, she'd struggled with knowing her time with Garrett and Micah was ending soon.

But with this latest news, it was clear the danger wasn't over yet. Unknown gunmen had shown up on the scene, likely hired by one of the other potential Woodward heirs.

There were so many gunmen in the area, she was surprised they weren't tripping over them.

Her phone vibrated, and she shifted her position to read the text from Garrett.

J.A. is hurt but we are ok. Call soon.

With one hand, she awkwardly typed a response.

Thanks for info.

It wasn't easy, sitting here in Garrett's office. She carefully shifted Micah to her other arm, shaking the numbness from her dominant limb.

"Do you need me to take him?" Liam must have noticed her discomfort. He smiled. "I have a daughter of my own."

"Maybe just for a minute, to use the restroom." She handed the baby over, then stood, stretching out her back. "I wish I could go talk to Garrett and Wyatt."

"Not yet. They'll be updating me soon." Liam smiled down at Micah. "He's a cute kid."

After using the restroom and splashing cold water on her face to help keep her awake, she returned to the office. Liam looked extremely comfortable with a baby in his arms. For a moment, she wondered about his wife, how she felt knowing her husband and the father of her daughter put his life on the line every day to keep the community safe.

No, what she really wondered was how *she* might handle it, if she were in that position. A ridiculous thought because she wasn't in a relationship with a cop. Garrett had a life and career here in Green Lake.

And her mission was to serve pregnant women in need, especially those who still lived on the Oneida reservation.

"Thanks." She took Micah from Liam. "Are you sure we can't head over there?"

He arched a brow. "I'm sure I'm not willing to take the risk. Micah is still in danger—now more than ever since we know Abernathy claimed to want him alive. And the new players may not feel the same way."

She sighed and dropped back into Garrett's chair. "Okay. You're right. It's just difficult to sit here, doing nothing."

"I understand." Liam's gaze was sympathetic.

Her phone vibrated again, this time with an incoming call. She quickly answered. "Garrett?"

"I'm okay," he assured her. "But Abernathy's sidekick was murdered, and he took a bullet to the upper chest. Thankfully, he was still alive when the ambulance carted him off."

"I heard from Liam." Although there had been no mention of Abernathy's dead cohort in crime. "Do you have any idea who is responsible?"

"Only theories at this point." Garrett sighed. "Once the medical examiner and crime scene techs get here, we'll head back. We found a vehicle nearby that we believe is Abernathy's. When the techs get here, we'll search the interior for additional information."

"Maybe Abernathy was staying in one of the local motels," she said. "He may have items in his room, too."

"Yes, Wyatt is working on that. It's late, though, so not sure we'll have that intel until morning."

"Understood." The crime scene techs were getting a work-out: first, processing Garrett's log home and now this. She doubted they were used to this much crime, especially over a short time frame.

Hopefully, they were up to the task and wouldn't miss anything.

"I'll call when we're on our way back," Garrett said. "How's Micah?"

"He's great. Sleeping." She yawned. "I'm feeling the late hour myself."

"We'll find a place to spend the rest of the night. Hang in there." She heard the murmur of voices, then Garrett said, "I'll talk to you soon."

"Bye." She set the phone on the desk and rested her head back against the chair. No matter how tired she was, she didn't dare fall asleep, fearing she might accidentally drop Micah.

Being up like this gave her a new appreciation for what new mothers went through while tending their newborns. The chance she hadn't had with Willow.

Remembering her daughter didn't give her the same pang of grief as it had previously. Maybe she was too exhausted to feel anything.

Or maybe she was too preoccupied with Micah, the baby who needed her now.

Willow would always have a piece of her heart. But for the first time, it occurred to her that there was room in her heart to love more babies.

Maybe even another baby of her own.

Garrett had found an ID in the pocket of Abernathy's dead sidekick. His name was Kevin Carter, and the address listed on the driver's license was Chicago.

He showed it to Wyatt. "None of the other gunmen have had IDs in their pockets, but this guy does."

Wyatt scowled. "We know there are more players in the game, but the guy you caught claimed Abernathy hired him. And he didn't have an ID on him."

"Right." The contradiction nagged at him. Garrett glanced around the clearing, lit up by the headlights of cars driven by the crime scene techs. "Maybe this Kevin Carter was a friend of Abernathy's. Rather than a hired gun."

"Or he was a bodyguard," Wyatt suggested.

"Could be. I was too far away to see what happened, but he may have tried to protect Abernathy."

Wyatt nodded, taking the ID and placing it in an evidence bag. "I'll ask Dispatch to run this guy, see if anything pops."

"A criminal record would be nice," Garrett agreed. "Then we'd know he was involved."

Wyatt made the call. When finished, he gestured behind them. "Let's go check on the vehicle they left down the road."

"I hope they left something useful behind." He was growing frustrated with the way every lead seemed to disintegrate before their eyes. Even learning the identity of Abernathy's sidekick wasn't helpful.

The vehicle was a black SUV but did not have tinted windows—more evidence that there were other gunmen involved. As if the shots fired at Abernathy and Carter weren't enough of a clue.

Using his flashlight, he peered in through the windows, being careful not to touch anything. There was a laptop case on the floor in the front passenger seat, and he shined the flashlight beam on it. "What do you think? Would he really have gone through with giving me the cash?"

"Doubtful. But I'd like to check the bag," Wyatt said. "Let's see if we can free up a crime scene tech to get inside.

As long as we don't disturb any fingerprints, it should be fine to check the bag."

The way things were going, Garrett didn't hold out much hope of finding anything useful. This case had been frustrating from the beginning, with no end in sight. Normally good, methodical police work paid off. The steady stream of gunmen was an aberration. Remembering what Liz had mentioned, he added, "We need to find which hotel they were using. It's more likely they left key documents there rather than in the car."

"Agreed, but that's no easy task in the height of tourist season," Wyatt drawled. "There's been more crime in the past few months than we've had all year."

"Tell me about it." Garrett sighed. "But now we have two names to question the hotels about. Abernathy likely secured the rooms under Kevin Carter's name rather than his."

"Good point." Wyatt gestured for a tech to join them. "We'd like to check inside that laptop case."

The tech sighed but didn't argue. Garrett had taken the key fob from Abernathy's pocket, and the tech used it now, through the evidence bag, to unlock the vehicle.

Using gloved hands, Wyatt carefully opened the door, trying not to smudge potential prints, then reached for the bag. He set it on the ground and unzipped it to look inside.

Garrett hunkered down beside him. There was a laptop inside. When they opened it, the screen was password protected, so Wyatt closed it again. Then he checked the inside pockets for any documents.

There was nothing inside. Not even a business card. Garrett swallowed a stab of disappointment. "Looks like finding their hotel is our priority."

"Right." Wyatt zipped up the laptop case, then set it back

on the floor where he'd found it. "Thanks for letting us take a look. We'll need to get that laptop to the computer experts to see what they can find."

"We will." The tech closed the car door. "Anything else?"

"No, but thanks." It was useless to hang around here much longer. And since the hour was going on one o'clock in the morning, Garrett figured their time would be better spent searching for the hotel.

Or getting some badly needed sleep.

His mind rejected the latter, but his body was slowing down, thanks to the adrenaline crash that washed over him.

"Let's head back to headquarters," Wyatt suggested. "We'll update Liam and go from there."

"Okay." He turned to walk back to the cabin. "But I need to get the baby carrier. It's the only bed we have for Micah."

It didn't take long for him to pick up the carrier and follow Wyatt to the location where he'd left his vehicle. The rental SUV would need to stay put until it had been cleared by the crime scene techs.

He brooded over the way the events had unfolded, wondering if there was anything he could have done differently. Nothing came to mind, especially considering Abernathy's demand he lift the baby to prove he was there.

"Abernathy expected this to be a trap." He glanced at Wyatt. "I'm surprised he didn't have more gunmen with him."

"Well, to be fair, you eliminated two of them," Wyatt said with a wry grin. The highway was deserted, so they were making good time. "Likely, he was low on resources."

"Maybe." Garrett yawned, then gave himself a mental shake. They needed answers, and waiting until morning didn't sit well. "I'll call hotels when we get to the station.

Maybe you could take Liz and Micah to your place for the night."

"I think it's a good idea to have all three of you stay at our place. Abby's at the hospital with Abernathy, and I don't think Liz and Micah should be alone."

"Right." Garrett winced. "I should have thought of that."

A few minutes later, Wyatt pulled into the parking lot outside their headquarters. As Garrett removed the baby carrier from the back seat, he realized this was where it had all started at least for him. The crack of gunfire had nearly struck him, Liz and Micah.

Mostly him, if he remembered correctly. Had that been Abernathy's first attempt? Had the goal been to kill him, then get to Micah? They wouldn't be able to interview Rebecca's former fiancé until he'd recovered from his surgery.

If he survived at all.

When they headed inside, he belatedly realized he'd forgotten to text Liz. She came out of his office, holding Micah, her beautiful green eyes wide with hope. "Did you find anything helpful?"

"Not yet." He hated to disappoint her. After setting the baby carrier down on the closest desk, he reached for his son. "Thanks for watching over him."

"Of course." She managed a tired smile. "He's a content baby."

He bent to kiss Micah's head, then glanced up as Liam entered. Deciding it was time to give Liz a break from holding him, he gently set Micah in the baby carrier "We pulled a laptop case from Abernathy's car, but there was nothing inside but a computer. We'll need the techs to get through the password protection for more intel."

Liam nodded. "You look beat. Get some sleep. There will be more work to be done in the morning."

"I just need to make a few calls first." He shot a guilty glance at Liz. "Do you mind waiting a little longer?"

"No problem." Her fatigued expression belied her words. "Can I help?"

"Try to get some rest. I'm hoping this won't take long. There is a limited number of hotels in Green Lake." To be fair, there were literally dozens of rental properties, but he was hoping those had been booked well in advance for the peak summer months, leaving Abernathy to take whatever low-budget hotel rooms might be available.

"Okay." She took the closest chair and rested her head on the desk near Micah's baby carrier. Squelching a flash of guilt, Garrett took a seat at the next desk over and booted up the computer. He decided to call the hotels in alphabetical order, as they were displayed online.

"I'll work on the search warrant," Wyatt said as he picked up the phone. "Judge Henry won't give us too much trouble, based on the facts at hand."

"Thanks." He started with Apple Grove Inn, giving his name and badge number before requesting guest information on Joel Abernathy or Kevin Carter. When he struck out there, he moved on to the next.

And the next.

The screen in front of him began to blur. He blinked the exhaustion away, trying to remain focused. He slowly, painstakingly made his way down the list until he reached the last one.

Woodland Escape Motel.

It wasn't *Woodward*, but the similarity gave him a glimmer of hope. He called the number and waited for several long rings before a grouchy guy answered. "Woodland Escape."

He quickly introduced himself as Chief Deputy Nichols. "I'm looking for a guest by the name of Kevin Carter."

"Do you know what time it is?" Annoyance laced the guy's tone. "Hang on."

Garrett rubbed his eyes. If Carter wasn't there, he'd give up for the night. They could tackle the rental properties in the morning.

"Yeah, he's here in Room 8. Why?"

"He's there?" Garrett struggled to focus. "Right now?"

"I mean, he *rented* Room 8," the guy clarified. "I haven't seen him. He's not due to check out until the end of the weekend."

Garrett had to pinpoint the day of the week. Today was Wednesday. No—technically, early Thursday. "Okay, we'll be there in a few minutes with a search warrant. Do not go into the room, do you understand? I don't want anything touched."

"A search warrant? At this hour?" The grumpy guy seemed more upset over losing sleep. Not that Garrett could really blame him.

"Yes." He clicked on the map to pinpoint the exact location of the Woodland Escape Motel. "You're five miles outside town, right? We'll be there in seven minutes or so."

"Hurry up, then," the guy groused before hanging up.

"We got a hit. They're at the Woodland Escape." Garrett surged to his feet, renewed with energy. "Did you wake the judge for the warrant?"

"Yep. He sent it electronically." For being in his midsixties, Judge Henry had adapted well to current technology.

"Let's go." Garrett turned toward the door, but Liz's voice stopped him.

"Can we ride along?" She blinked the sleep from her eyes and reached for Micah's baby carrier.

Liam had gone home, so he glanced at Wyatt, who shrugged. "Better we stick together."

"Sure, but you'll need to stay in the car." Garrett took the heavy carrier from her hand. "Try to get some sleep while you wait."

"I'm okay." She yawned, then smiled. "Well, I'm as okay as you are."

He couldn't help but chuckle as he secured Micah's carrier in Wyatt's SUV. Liz climbed into the back with the baby, leaving Garrett and Wyatt to sit up front.

When they reached the hotel, they drove around the building, checking things out before pulling into the small parking lot. There were several vehicles parked but a few open spaces, too. It occurred to him that other gunmen might be staying there, but you couldn't get a search warrant that would allow them to knock on every single motel-room door.

Still, the way Wyatt glanced at him indicated they were on the same page. They exited the vehicle, then headed inside.

An older gentleman with shock-white hair stood waiting for them. When Garrett flashed his badge and Wyatt showed him the warrant on his phone, he thrust the key card at them. "Take it and hurry up. I'd like to get back to bed."

"Thanks." Garrett took the key and turned to walk back outside. Wyatt stayed close beside him.

After knocking on the door without a response, Garrett used the key to get inside. The room was empty, as he'd expected. It was messy, as if there hadn't been room service lately.

"Here." Wyatt had opened the top dresser drawer with a gloved hand. "There's an envelope."

Garrett's pulse kicked up as he carefully opened the metal clasp. He was wearing gloves, too, but still tried to handle the contents carefully.

What he saw made him gasp. "It's a marriage certificate."

Wyatt leaned over his shoulder, then whistled. "No wonder he wanted the kid."

The document claimed Joel T. Abernathy was legally married to Rebecca M. Woodward as of one month ago.

A secret wedding? Or a fake marriage license? As there was no record online about a marriage, his gut leaned toward the latter.

He could only pray the truth wouldn't die with Abernathy.

FOURTEEN

A noise woke Liz from her nap. She lifted her head, wincing at the pain in her neck. It took a moment for her to realize she'd fallen asleep in the SUV, with her head against the window at an awkward angle. No wonder her neck hurt. Glancing at Micah, she noticed he was squirming in his seat.

"Hey there, it's okay." She reached over to unbuckle the straps holding him in place, stifling a yawn. The short nap had not put much of a dent in her level of exhaustion.

She lifted Micah to her shoulder, nuzzling him for a moment before setting him down on her lap to change him. She quickly prepared a bottle, then offered it to Micah. Glancing outside, she watched as Garrett and Wyatt emerged from the motel room, their expressions grim.

There was a large tan envelope in Garrett's hand. A surge of adrenaline jolted her fully awake.

They'd found something!

Garrett must have sensed she was looking at him, because he quickly strode toward her. He opened the car door, his expression softening when he saw his son.

"What is that?" She nodded at the envelope.

"A marriage certificate."

"What?" Had she heard that correctly? "Whose marriage certificate?"

He turned so she could read both Rebecca's and Joel's names on the document.

She gasped. "No way."

"Yeah, that was my first thought, too. I hope it's fake, but what if it isn't?" He shrugged. "Then it looks like I'll have to fight Abernathy for custody of Micah. Hopefully, once he's arrested, the judge will grant me custody as Micah's biological father, considering Abernathy is facing charges. But I'm not familiar with family law to know if that will be enough. And I know DNA testing to prove Rebecca's deathbed statement that I'm his father will take some time." He shrugged wearily. "My biggest concern is being able to keep Micah with me while this issue works its way through the court system."

Fatigue made it difficult to think clearly. "When Rebecca came to my clinic, she didn't say anything about being recently married. And I saw an engagement ring, not a wedding ring."

Garrett frowned. "You know, now that I think back, I don't remember seeing an engagement ring when we found her body in my bedroom. Not that that fact alone means much. Abernathy will claim both rings were stolen. Who knows? Maybe that was why he scooped up her body from your clinic in the first place. Well, that and using it to try to frame me for her murder."

The lengths Abernathy had taken were staggering. "All because he wanted control over the Woodward fortune." She shook her head, looking down at Micah's innocent features. His dark eyes were open and looking up at her. She smiled and bent to kiss his forehead. What was it about babies that made them so kissable?

"Yeah, and he clearly planned to do whatever was necessary to get it." Garrett sighed. "Time for us to drive back to headquarters. I want to get this evidence locked up. Then we'll find a place to sleep for what's left of the night."

Wyatt came over to join them. "I sent another officer to the hospital to relieve Abby. We agreed that we'd like the three of you to stay with us. At least for tonight. She'll meet us at home soon."

Garrett frowned. "I don't want to put you both in danger."

Wyatt arched a brow. "Pretty sure with three deputies in the house, we can handle anything that comes up. Besides, this way, we can head over to the hospital first thing tomorrow to interview Abernathy."

"Yeah, but I can guarantee he'll claim the marriage was real," Garrett groused. "He has nothing to lose and everything to gain."

"He'll end up spending the rest of his life in jail," Wyatt said confidently. "And the DNA will prove you're Micah's father. Don't borrow trouble. Let's take this one day at a time."

"I agree with Wyatt." Liz held Micah up against her shoulder so he could burp. "Abernathy claimed he'd pay you for Micah. It's doubtful he planned on following through." She abruptly scowled. "I'd like to know exactly who shot him."

"I vote that it's someone from the Woodward family," Wyatt said. "Unless one of his gunmen decided to turn against him for some reason."

The brief spurt of adrenaline had faded, leaving her feeling shaky and more tired than ever before. "Can we talk about this tomorrow?"

"Yeah, that's for the best. We'll drop off this evidence, then take Wyatt and Abby up on their offer." Garrett stepped back and closed the door.

As the two men climbed into the front seat, she settled Micah back in his baby carrier. The trip back wouldn't take long, but she didn't want to risk more bad guys popping up out of nowhere, forcing them into another car chase.

Better to keep Micah safe in his car seat.

She'd almost nodded off again but jerked awake when they arrived. Wyatt slid out of the passenger seat and ran inside with the tan envelope. He returned a few minutes later, then proceeded to give Garrett instructions on how to get to his home.

Abby and Wyatt's house was smaller than Garrett's log cabin, but they had two guest rooms, which worked perfectly.

"I can keep Micah in my room," she offered.

"He's my son. I'll take care of him." There was a hint of testiness in his tone. They were all tired and crabby, so she didn't take offense.

"Just remember, this isn't over yet," Wyatt cautioned. "We still don't know who shot Abernathy. We need you at your best if we run across more danger."

Garrett frowned. "Micah is my responsibility."

"He should sleep for a few hours now," she said, gently taking the carrier from him. "Why not keep him with me? If he wakes up again, I'll take care of him, then leave him with you for a bit."

Garrett reluctantly nodded. "Okay, thank you."

"Anytime." She carried Micah into her room and set him on the floor beside the bed. Then she gratefully crawled in and closed her eyes.

As she drifted off to sleep, a surge of sadness washed over her, knowing this was probably the last night she'd have with Garrett and Micah before heading back to her lonely life.

One that didn't seem as noble as it had when she'd initially opened her clinic.

Selfishly, she wanted more.

* * *

Garrett awoke at eight o'clock in the morning, feeling refreshed after a solid five hours of sleep. He glanced around but didn't see Micah.

He quickly showered and changed into clothes Wyatt had provided, then went to find his son. The soft cries coming from Liz's room made him open the door quickly.

Liz was awake, though, blinking the sleep from her eyes. She glanced at him, then at Micah. "He slept this whole time!"

"He did? That's wonderful!" He was glad she'd been able to get some rest, too. "I'll take him."

"Thanks." She gazed at Micah for a moment before he grabbed the baby and the diaper bag. He gave her some privacy, following the enticing scent of coffee to the kitchen.

Abby was up, drinking coffee at the table. "I didn't hear him cry once last night."

"Me, either. I think five hours is a record," he joked.

"Wyatt is in the shower. He'll join us soon. We can make a plan over breakfast."

He liked the sound of that. He changed Micah, then fed him while sipping coffee. He tried not to stress over the idea of the court not granting him custody.

One step at a time, he reminded himself.

When Liz joined them, his heart thudded against his ribs. It wasn't just her beauty that got to him but also the way she bravely faced the danger stalking them while keeping Micah safe from harm.

She was an amazing woman, and despite how much he'd cared for Rebecca, he found himself wishing for a chance to spend more time with Liz once this was over.

Yet the distance between them, not to mention their unpredictable schedules, would make any sort of relationship nearly impossible.

And not a priority, he told himself sternly. Not now. Not until they got to the bottom of this.

"I can help with breakfast," Liz said when Abby began pulling food from the fridge.

"Sit." Abby waved her back. "After everything you've been through, you deserve to relax a bit."

"I can help." Wyatt came into the kitchen, pausing to give his wife a quick kiss before joining her at the sink.

Cherishing this time with his son, he couldn't seem to tear his gaze from his sweet, innocent face.

It was inconceivable that anyone could look at this baby and see dollar signs rather than the blessed beginning of a new life. He silently prayed they would uncover the truth today so that this innocent baby would no longer be in the center of danger.

Liz, too, deserved to have her life back. He felt guilty over knowing her patients couldn't get the care they needed until this was over.

The scent of bacon and eggs filled the kitchen. The way Wyatt and Abby worked as a team made him all the more aware of Liz sitting beside him. She'd been a rock through all this. He wouldn't have made it through these early days with his son without her.

When the meal was ready, he put Micah back in his baby carrier so they could eat. Wyatt took the lead in saying grace.

"Dear Lord, we thank You for this food we are about to eat. We are grateful for everything You've done for us and continue to seek Your care and guidance as we uncover the truth. Amen."

"Amen," the three of them added in unison.

"What's the plan?" Abby asked. "Other than interviewing Abernathy once he's able to talk?"

"I called Deputy Owens at the hospital. He informed me

that Abernathy is out of surgery and is considered medically stable. He's heavily medicated, so not sure how much we'll get out of him," Wyatt informed them.

"I was afraid of that." Garrett sighed. "And if he is medicated, we can't question him while he's under the influence of pain meds."

"We can still ask if he saw who shot him," Abby pointed out. "That's different than asking him to incriminate himself in his plot to buy Micah."

"Maybe." Garrett wasn't a lawyer, but he'd been involved in enough cases to know they were treading on dangerous ground. "As long as we make it clear we're only trying to find the man who shot him and his bodyguard."

"Why don't you let me and Abby take the lead on that?" Wyatt suggested. "You should probably track down information on the marriage certificate we found in Abernathy's motel room."

"Okay." Letting them take the interview was going against the grain. Normally, he didn't have trouble delegating duties; that was a big part of his role as chief deputy. But it was his son who was in danger, and he preferred to be involved in each step of the investigation.

Yet he also doubted Abernathy would give them much of anything to go on. Even if their intent was to find out who shot him, the guy may still refuse to cooperate.

Maybe his time would be better spent here.

"I'll take Liz and Micah to headquarters to work. I need to fill Liam in on what happened."

"Sounds good," Abby agreed.

Liz nodded but didn't say much. She seemed more quiet than usual.

When they'd finished eating, Liz jumped up to help with

the dishes. He joined her, shooing Wyatt and Abby away. "We've got this. You should hit the road."

They exchanged a look, then Wyatt nodded. "Okay. The sooner we get out there, the better."

"We'll lock up when we leave," Garrett added.

"That's fine." Abby waved her hand. "You could stay here to work, too, if that's more comfortable for taking care of the baby."

She had a point. "We'll see how it goes." He kept his response noncommittal. While he could easily talk to Liam over the phone, he didn't feel comfortable staying here without Abby and Wyatt. Hanging around their personal space felt like an invasion of their privacy.

Not that they would take it that way. He'd been leaning on the couple as friends when he was really their boss. Normally, he wouldn't cross the line like this.

But these were exigent circumstances. He would do that and more to protect Liz and his son.

"Do you really think you can prove the marriage certificate is fake?" Liz glanced at him, washing the dishes while he dried them.

"I honestly don't know. Wyatt said there was nothing on file with the state. But that could take time, too. I still think he faked Rebecca's signature with the intent on filing it later." He paused, then added, "The same way we were going to fake Micah's death."

"Yeah, I've been thinking of that, too." She sighed. "It won't be easy to prove her signature is fake. Especially if he somehow convinced her to sign under duress."

"I know." The more he thought about the document, the more concerned he was about how he'd fight to keep Micah.

"We have to trust that God has a plan," Liz murmured.

"You're right." He felt a flash of shame. "I won't lose

faith. God sent Rebecca to you for a reason. She must have found your clinic online and thought you were her best option for delivering Micah in secret."

"Exactly," she agreed.

"I have to believe God won't fail to protect and guide us now."

A smile tugged at the corner of her mouth. "I wish there was something I could do to help. Maybe we should find a handwriting expert. He might be able to figure out if the signature is fake or was written under duress."

"It's possible." He had enough experience with court cases to know that for every expert to testify on one end of the spectrum, there was another expert who could annihilate that same theory.

"Are you planning to stay here?" she asked.

He dried the last dish, then turned to face her. "No. I'd rather go to headquarters to work. I know it would be more comfortable for you to take care of Micah here, but I don't want to abuse Abby and Wyatt's hospitality." He hesitated before adding, "We may need to stay here again tonight."

"I understand. Don't worry about me and Micah." She turned to glance at the baby. "We're fine sticking around the sheriff's department for as long as you need to work."

"Thanks. I appreciate that." He draped the damp dish towel over the handle of the dishwasher. "Give me a few minutes, then we'll head out."

"Sounds good." She crossed over to the table and began packing Micah's diaper bag.

He quickly made the bed in his room. When he paused outside the door to glance inside the guest room Liz had used, he found she'd already taken care of it.

Returning to the kitchen, he picked up Micah's baby carrier. "Ready to go?"

She nodded but stopped short when his phone rang. He fished it out from his pocket, then set Micah back on the table. "It's Liam," he explained before answering.

"Garrett?" Liam's voice sounded curt. "Where are you?"

His muscles tensed. "At Wyatt and Abby's place. Why? What's going on?"

"Wyatt thinks he may have picked up a tail. He wanted me to warn the two of you to be careful."

Goose bumps rippled along his skin as he met Liz's gaze. If the gunmen knew enough about Wyatt and Abby, they weren't safe here. "Okay, thanks for letting us know about the tail. We're getting out of here now. We planned to come to headquarters."

"Stay put, I'll have two deputies come out to meet you," Liam said.

"Okay, that's fine." He'd no sooner disconnected from the call when he heard the crack of gunfire. "Down!"

Instead of ducking down, Liz placed her body over Micah's baby carrier. As much as he was touched by her attempt to protect him, he pulled on her arm and quickly grabbed the handle of his son's carrier. He placed it beneath the oak table, then pulled Liz down to join him.

Another crack of gunfire shattered a second window. How many shooters were there? More than one, since a window on either side of the house had been broken.

And they were stuck in the middle.

"We need to move," he told Liz. "Follow me."

Her green eyes were wide with fear and determination as she nodded.

The center island had a granite-stone top, and there was a slight overhang on all sides. He wanted to be on the inside of the island, sandwiched between the two sets of cabinets.

He grabbed Micah's carrier, then crawled with the baby

out from the table and darted around the island. Liz followed close behind.

Another round of gunfire reverberated through the room. He tucked Liz and Micah as far beneath the granite overhang as possible, then pulled his weapon.

Lifting his head, he tried to pinpoint the location of the shooters. No easy task, since he didn't want to leave Liz or Micah unattended.

Liz pulled out her phone and called 911. He listened to her explain the situation as he watched through the now broken window for signs of the gunmen.

A flash of movement caught his eye. He instinctively fired at the spot, grateful when he saw the guy hit the ground. He wasn't sure he'd hit him, but he'd pinned him down, which was almost as good.

A gunshot from the other side of the house echoed loudly. He didn't hear a window shatter, so he hoped the perp had missed. But at this rate, it wouldn't take long for these guys to force their way inside.

Come on, Liam, get our deputies out here!

Micah began to cry, a sound that ripped at his heart. Liz tried to soothe the infant as he continued keeping watch.

A thumping sound drew his attention. One of the gunmen had gotten inside the house!

Garrett edged toward the corner of the island. When he saw the shadow of the guy on the wall, he jumped out from the corner and fired two quick shots in a row.

The perp fired back, the bullet imbedding into the wall beside him, missing his head by an inch. Then the perp he'd struck slid to the floor.

One down, one to go.

The wail of sirens indicated his backup was close. He could hear Liz whispering the Lord's Prayer as he inched forward to kick the perp's weapon out of the way and check for a pulse.

He was alive, but based on the chest wound, he wasn't sure the perp would make it.

"Who sent you?" He lifted the guy's head. "Come on, tell me who sent you!"

"Ebber…" The guy slumped sideways. And this time, when Garrett felt for a pulse, there was nothing.

A wave of frustration took over. What had the guy said? Edward? Elaine? Or someone else?

FIFTEEN

Curling her body over Micah's carrier, Liz silently prayed for safety. She couldn't believe more gunmen had shown up at Wyatt and Abby's house. Their quest to kill Micah was relentless.

She couldn't help but wonder if the innocent baby would ever be safe again. Right now, she held out little hope that they'd make it out of this nightmare unscathed.

"Garrett?" The deep male voice held an authoritative tone. "Is everyone okay?"

"Yes, thanks for getting here so quickly, Liam." Garrett came over to help her up from her crouched position under the granite slab of Wyatt's kitchen island. "One dead in here, but there's at least one other outside."

"The perp out here is down but alive. Stay put while we clear the area."

Liz's entire body was trembling, so staying put wasn't a hardship. She should be used to bullets flying by now.

But she wasn't. This was so outside her normal life of offering pre and postnatal care to her patients.

"Here, let me take Micah." Garrett gently eased her aside to lift the carrier from the floor and onto the table. Then he gathered the crying infant into his arms, holding him close. She sank into one of the kitchen chairs, trying to control her rapid pulse. No wonder stress was often a precursor to a heart attack. "What did the gunman say? Who hired him?"

Garrett frowned. "I'm not sure. He may have said *Edward* or *Elaine* or something else. I don't think we can put much stock in his mumbled attempt to answer my question."

She wanted to scream in frustration. They were no closer to figuring out who had masterminded these attacks—someone other than Abernathy, who was in the hospital.

After several long moments as Garrett soothed his son, she heard Liam's voice outside shouting, "All clear!"

A quick glance around Wyatt and Abby's home revealed several broken windows. She felt certain bullets would be found imbedded in the walls or furniture. It wasn't their fault, but she still felt guilty for the damage that had been done to their property.

"We shouldn't have come here." Garrett's low voice held regret.

She waved a hand at the mess. "You couldn't have anticipated this. Wyatt and Abby didn't, either."

"We should have." His expression hardened. "Whoever is behind this must know more about me than I realized."

She nodded slowly, understanding his concern. "Or they followed us here somehow. Maybe waited until they saw Wyatt and Abby leave before striking out."

"That's a reasonable assumption, too." Garrett gently set Micah back in his carrier as Liam entered the house. "How many were out there?"

"Just the one. He's still alive but has fallen unconscious. An ambulance is on the way." Liam scowled. "We couldn't get any information out of him."

"I didn't get anything from this guy, either." Garrett gestured to the dead gunman. "I know I'm supposed to hand you my badge and gun after shooting a man, but I can't do that until we find the mastermind behind this."

"I wasn't going to ask you for your shield or your weapon," Liam said mildly. "Our small community hasn't had this much violence in a long time. I need the help of every deputy in the department."

Garrett winced. "I know my leave of absence is causing you to be shorthanded."

"Since you're smack in the middle of this mess, it's almost like having you on duty." Liam's gaze softened when he looked at Micah. "You're doing a fine job of protecting your son."

"Am I?" Garrett looked somber. "It doesn't feel that way."

"We'll get to the bottom of this," Liam assured him. "We're eliminating the gunmen, which is a step in the right direction."

Liz wanted to believe Liam and his deputies would uncover the truth, but so far, it seemed as if they were still stumbling around in the dark. She struggled to remain calm and positive. "How are Wyatt and Abby? I heard you mention a tail. Was someone following them?"

Liam glanced at her. "Good question. I'll check in with them now."

She and Garrett listened as the sheriff used his radio to connect with Abby. "What's your twenty?"

"Still en route to the hospital," Abby responded. "We had to take a detour to lose our tail."

"I'm afraid two armed perps showed up at your place and shot out a few of your windows," Liam informed her.

"How are Garrett, Liz and the baby?" Abby quickly asked. "Anyone hurt?"

"Just the gunmen. One dead, the other on his way to the

hospital." Liam frowned. "You better watch your six. Those guys following you may try to beat you to the hospital."

"We've put Owens and the hospital security staff on notice for that," Abby said.

Liz understood they were concerned about another attempt to silence Joel Abernathy—permanently.

Garrett spoke up. "We'll board up the windows, and I'll pay for the repairs."

"Don't worry, it's part of the job. We're just glad no one was hurt." Abby didn't sound the least bit upset about the property damage. "We'll take care of it. You have your own house cleanup to deal with."

From the determination in Garrett's eyes, Liz knew he'd insist. Not that the property damage was their biggest concern.

Their sole mission was to stay alive.

Garrett must have read her thoughts. He glanced between her and the baby, then turned to Liam. "We need a safe house. And I'm running out of options."

"Let's drive to headquarters for now." Liam ran his hand through his dark hair. "I need to create a formal report about this. And you'll be safe inside the brick building."

Would they really? She forced the lingering doubt aside since it was likely their best option.

She turned when Micah began to fuss. No child should be in this tenuous position. She lifted the baby to her shoulder and bowed her head, resting her cheek on his downy, soft dark hair.

Garrett came up beside her, encircling her waist with his arm and squeezing her in a hug. Then he lifted his hand to stroke his son's back while pressing a kiss to her temple. In that brief moment, she felt as if they were a family.

As soon as the thought entered her mind, she thrust it

away. No matter how much she wanted this, she knew better than to read into Garrett's gratitude.

At some point, the danger would be over and their lives would go back to normal.

Her patients needed her. More than Garrett did.

Garrett wanted to kiss Liz, but Liam's presence held him back. Besides, he wasn't sure she'd welcome a kiss from him. Not after the way they'd constantly been in danger ever since meeting. His promise to keep her safe was failing miserably.

It was only through God's grace that they'd survived this latest attack. That, and the warning from Wyatt and Abby about being followed.

Too bad he didn't know of any bomb shelters in town. It felt as if that was about the only place he'd be able to keep Liz and Micah safe.

He forced himself to step back from Liz and Micah. "Does he need to eat before we go?"

"Yes, I think we need a few minutes." She cooed to Micah, swaying back and forth until the baby quieted. Then she gently placed him in the baby carrier, tucking the small white bunny close. "I think the gunfire hurt his ears. I'll make a bottle. Shouldn't take too long before we're ready to go."

"Take your time." He wanted to feed Micah himself, but he was determined to stay alert for more danger. He crossed over to the dead gunman. After donning gloves, he went through his pockets.

"Hey, Liam?" He drew out a wallet. "This guy has an ID."

"Let's see." Liam joined him. "Jacob Burns—and no surprise, his address is listed as Chicago, Illinois. Does that name ring a bell?"

"No." He wished it did. "Interesting this gunman had his ID when most of the others hadn't."

"Maybe he's not a professional. They could be running low on resources." Liam clicked on his radio. "Dispatch, run the name Jacob Burns through the system." He rattled off the guy's date of birth and address as listed on the driver's license.

"Ten-four."

A surge of excitement hit hard. This could be the break they were looking for.

He glanced over to where Liz was finishing Micah's bottle. She lifted the baby and sat with him in the crook of her arm. It was humbling how she'd set aside her grief over losing her daughter to care for his son.

The urge to pull her close was strong, but he forced himself to turn away. This was hardly the time to be thinking about how beautiful she was and how much he'd come to care for her.

Far more than he should.

He needed to stay focused on the threat lurking outside and the never-ending stream of armed perps stalking them, who were obviously determined to kill his son.

"Garrett?" Liz's voice broke into his thoughts.

"Do you need something?" He crossed over to rest his hand on his son's head.

"I was just thinking about that marriage certificate you found in Abernathy's motel room." She frowned. "Don't you think there would have been an announcement in the newspapers about the wedding? Even a small wedding in the courthouse would be big news."

"Good point. Abernathy might claim they wanted to keep things quiet, but that will look suspicious if he shows up with a baby and a marriage certificate that the rest of the family knew nothing about." Yet it occurred to him that the couple may have gotten married in a private ceremony because of Rebecca's father's cancer diagnosis. And if the marriage was real, his life was about to get complicated.

Still, Abernathy would be arrested for the role he'd played in hiring a man to shoot him. Could a good defense lawyer convince a jury that Abernathy was only desperate to get his own son?

Maybe. The problem with juries was that anything was possible.

His gut tightened at the thought of fighting for custody of his son. "As soon as Micah is finished, we'll go back to headquarters so I can dig into it further."

Liam's radio crackled. "Sheriff? We ran a check on Jacob Burns, but he doesn't have a criminal record."

"Thanks. See if you can broaden the search to family members. He's been killed, so we'll need to make a death notification."

"Will do."

"I pray he has family somewhere," Garrett said. "We need to know who hired him."

"Agreed." Liam glanced at Liz and Micah with a soft smile. "Reminds me of the early days with our daughter, Ciara. All she did was eat and sleep, but now she's more alert and smiling. Every day with her is a blessing."

"I hope I'm blessed the same way." He did his best to shake off the sense of doom. "It's hard to plan a future when I can't find a safe place to stay."

"We'll get to the bottom of this." Liam lightly clapped him on the shoulder. "Having an ID on the dead gunman is a good clue. I believe we'll find family that may be able to give us intel on what he was up to."

Garrett hoped his boss was right about that. He was anxious to get to headquarters to search for information.

While waiting for Micah to finish his bottle, he made

good on his promise to board up the windows with plywood he found in the basement.

"Good boy," Liz murmured, holding Micah up to her shoulder. She glanced at Garrett. "We should be able to leave soon."

"Great." He tried to hide his impatience. It wasn't like they weren't well protected here, with deputies outside and Liam nearby. Yet there was a deep sense of urgency pushing at him to get out of there as soon as possible.

He glanced at Liam, who stood off to the side, working on his phone. "Liam? Do you have something?"

His boss turned to face him. "Wyatt and Abby are at the hospital. Abernathy is refusing to speak to them without his attorney present."

That figured. "Does he realize how much danger he's in?"

A smile tugged at the corner of Liam's mouth. "They're doing their best to convince him to cooperate. Sounds like he's afraid of being hurt again but doesn't want to incriminate himself too much."

Garrett swallowed a wave of frustration. Time was of the essence, considering the recent attack. "I hope he gets his lawyer there ASAP."

"He will." Liam sounded confident. "He's upset they have one ankle cuffed to the bed."

"'Cuffed to the bed'?" Liz echoed. "Even when he's in the hospital?"

"Yes, that's what happens when you're under arrest." Garrett didn't have any sympathy to spare for Abernathy. Not after everything they'd been through.

Before Garrett could suggest heading out, Liam's radio crackled once more. Then he heard the dispatcher's voice say, "Sheriff? I have information on your perp, Jacob Burns."

"Go ahead, tell me what you have," Liam said.

"He has a wife, Alicia, and a ten-year-old daughter, Amelia. Looks like there are serious money issues there. I see there are some debt collections on file, with legal action pending, and it appears their house has very recently gone into foreclosure." The dispatcher paused, then added, "Do you want to interview her about this? It would make sense for you to handle the death notification at the same time."

"Yeah, I'll take care of it. Thanks for the additional information." Liam lowered his hand from the radio and turned to face Garrett. "Financial issues may explain why Burns took this job. Could be someone from Woodward Enterprises promised to pay off his loans, even going as far as to get his house out of the foreclosure process in exchange for eliminating Micah as the Woodward heir."

"Yeah, especially since Robert Woodward's company specializes in real estate. They could easily buy the mortgage out without breaking a sweat." It wasn't proof, but it was a link back to the Woodward family.

A very weak link.

His feelings must have shown on his face. "Yeah, I know, it's not much. But once Abernathy's lawyer gets there, we should learn more," Liam assured him. "He has every reason to cooperate with us."

Since it was about the only break they'd gotten, Garrett nodded. "I pray you're right about that."

He glanced over to see that Liz had finished feeding and changing Micah. "Are you ready to go?" he asked.

"Yes." Her smile was strained. "I can't deny I'll be glad to get out of here."

"I'll escort you, Liz and Micah to headquarters," Liam offered.

"Thanks, we're ready." He watched as Liz placed Micah

in his carrier. He crossed over to clean the bottle and put the formula back in the diaper bag, then looped the strap over his shoulder. He lifted Micah's carrier from the table. "Lead the way, Liam."

"You got it." His boss reached for his radio. "Make sure there's a clear path to the SUVs."

"Roger that," came the response.

Liam led the way outside. Garrett urged Liz to follow, holding Micah's carrier high in front of him to protect the baby with his body. Thankfully, covering the short distance to the SUV was uneventful.

"I'll follow you," Liam said. "My goal will be to prevent you from picking up a tail the way Abby and Wyatt did."

"I appreciate that." As he belted Micah's carrier in the rear passenger seat, the back of his neck prickled. Almost as if someone was out there, watching.

Waiting for the opportunity to strike.

Reminding himself the deputies had cleared the area, he ignored the sensation. Liz was already tucked up front, and Liam stood a few paces back, covering them.

He stepped back and shut the door. As he rounded the back of the SUV, he swept another glance around the area but saw nothing alarming.

Once he was seated behind the wheel, Liam hustled over to the other SUV. Garrett started the engine, then headed out of Wyatt and Abby's driveway.

Liam followed close behind.

Five miles wasn't that far, but the winding highway roads made it difficult to go any faster than thirty miles per hour. He also didn't want to lose Liam or create too much of a gap between them.

As he took one corner, he heard a loud popping sound.

"What was that?" Liz asked fearfully.

"I don't know." He glanced in the rearview mirror, expecting to see Liam coming up behind him, but the stretch of highway behind him was empty.

Then he heard another sharp crack. The wheel beneath his hands jerked, the SUV swerving back and forth, then listing to one side.

They'd been hit!

His right rear tire had been struck by a bullet—no easy task, even for a professional. The realization that this was exactly how these guys had gotten to Rebecca flashed in his mind. Garrett managed to get the SUV off the road. He pulled his weapon but then froze as two men dressed in black came rushing toward them. They split up so they were positioned on either side of his vehicle—one outside his driver's-side window and the other on Liz's side. And each man had their weapon trained directly at them.

From this distance, they couldn't miss.

"Drop the gun and get out, now!" one of them shouted.

Garrett knew that he could probably take out one of the gunmen but not both.

They were trapped!

SIXTEEN

A strange sense of calm washed over Liz as she stared at the muzzle of the gunman's weapon mere inches from the passenger-side window. She, Garrett and Micah were about to die. And as awful as that was, she was at peace with her relationship with Jesus.

Oh, she didn't want to die. Especially knowing Micah would leave this earth, too, before he'd even had a chance to live. But it seemed as if God was calling them home, regardless of her wishes.

She couldn't tear her gaze from the lethal weapon. As if staring at it would somehow keep the gunman from shooting her in the face.

Garrett sat rigidly tense beside her. She almost blurted out how much she loved him when she heard a shout.

"Police! Drop your weapons!"

Fueled by a sudden burst of anger, she abruptly threw her door open, catching the gunman off guard as the frame slammed into his weapon. As if they'd choreographed the move, Garrett did the same on his side.

More gunfire rang out, along with the shatter of glass, causing Micah to cry. The poor baby had been in far too many dangerous situations in his short life.

She ducked behind the now open door, using it as a shield. Then the gunfire abruptly stopped.

Tentatively lifting her head, she searched the area. The man who'd been standing on her side of the vehicle was lying on the ground.

Turning, she looked at Garrett. He still had his weapon trained toward his broken window. There was no sign of the gunman, but that didn't mean he was dead.

"Two perps down," Liam shouted. "Stay where you are."

Liz lowered her chin to her chest, reverently thanking God for saving them again.

Especially for protecting Micah. An innocent child who had been targeted for elimination because of greed.

"This one's wounded," Liam said, coming up on her side. "Garrett, your guy is down. Check him out."

Garrett slid out from behind the wheel. "This guy is dead. I took him out with a head shot."

"I can help the wounded man." She stood on shaky legs, then rounded the open door to kneel behind the man she believed had been seconds from killing her. He was young, his features vaguely familiar.

Liam had shot him high along the left side of his chest, an injury that reminded her of the way Rebecca had been wounded. She balled up his shirt and applied pressure to the opening. "Call an ambulance," she said. Then she added, "Garrett, does this guy look familiar to you?"

Garrett came around the front of the vehicle and kneeled on the injured man's other side. "Yeah. He's Jeremy Woodward."

Jeremy? It took a moment for her to place him as Edward's son. "Do you think his father sent him?"

"I do." Garrett scowled. "Edward isn't the type to get his hands dirty."

"Ambulance is on the way," Liam assured her. "Is there anything I can do to help?"

"Not yet." She prayed Jeremy wouldn't die, fearing they'd never know the truth about whether he was working alone or was in cahoots with his family. Leaning her weight on one hand covering the wound, she used the other to check for a pulse. "He's still with us."

"Good." She could tell Garrett wanted this guy to live as much as she did. The sound of vehicles arriving made her glance over her shoulder. Several deputy squads had arrived, likely coming from the scene at Wyatt and Abby's house.

She wanted to believe the danger was over. But the relentless attacks indicated Edward could keep hiring men to come after them if they didn't come up with some proof of his culpability soon.

As deputies swarmed the area, Garrett pulled Micah from his carrier and comforted the crying baby. Her heart swelled with love at the sight of them. He'd come a long way from their initial meeting, when he'd avoided holding his son.

In the moments she'd believed they would all die at the hands of the assailants, she'd realized just how much she loved Garrett. Especially his strength, kindness and integrity. Not that she expected him to feel the same way. She would miss him—and Micah, too—once it was safe enough to return to seeing patients in her clinic.

The ambulance arrived a few minutes later. She didn't let up on the pressure until they'd started an IV and began infusing fluids. Finally, she moved back, giving the EMTs room to work.

"Here." Garrett handed her a few baby wipes from Micah's diaper bag to clean Jeremy's blood from her hands. "Are you okay? You're not hurt?"

"Fine." She managed a smile. "I couldn't believe you opened your door into the gunman at the exact same time I did."

"I was surprised, too," he admitted. "I didn't dare take the time to tell you to do the same. My hope was that Liam would take care of your gunman, leaving me to handle the guy on my side of the car."

"It worked." She took a step toward him, as if drawn by an invisible wire. "I fully expected us to die here today."

"The possibility flashed through my mind." To her surprise, he reached out and drew her closer. "I prayed Liam would get here in time to help."

She leaned against him, burrowing her face into the hollow of his shoulder. Micah was awake and looking up at his father with an intense gaze.

Tears pricked her eyes. She silently acknowledged she had no desire to go back to her former life. Granted, she liked helping mothers in need, but leaving Garrett and Micah would be incredibly difficult.

"Hey, I just heard from Wyatt and Abby." Liam's voice broke into her thoughts. "We need to join them at the hospital ASAP. One of the perps is ready to talk."

"Abernathy?" Garrett asked.

"No, the other guy you wounded, the one who left the scene of the shooting in Volver County. Was that yesterday? I'm losing track." Liam sighed. "We'll take one of these vehicles, leaving the deputies on scene to take care of our damaged SUVs."

"Are you okay to leave?" Garrett asked her.

"Of course." It was ironic how accustomed she'd come to being under fire. "I'm all for finding out if this guy can give us answers."

Garrett surprised her by pulling her close and giving

her a kiss. The embrace was all too brief, but she felt the impact of his kiss all the way down to the tips of her toes.

Then he stepped back to address Liam. "Let's go."

She took the diaper bag as Garrett grabbed Micah's carrier. This wasn't the time or the place to tell him how she felt. How much she loved him.

Not until the danger was over for good.

Those tense moments of being trapped by two gunmen had aged Garrett ten years. Yet a surge of adrenaline hit with the thought of getting information from one of the hired thugs who'd come after him and Micah.

He rode up front with Liam, leaving Liz and Micah in the back. He watched as she leaned over, gently caressing Micah's head as she tucked the stuffed bunny closer to the baby.

Liz was the only mother Micah had ever known. When they'd faced what seemed to be certain death, his biggest regret was not telling her how much he loved her.

Soon, though, he silently promised. He wasn't sure how they'd make a relationship work with the distance between them, but he was determined to try.

Even if that meant applying for a job with the Green Bay Police Department, since that would bring him much closer to where her clinic was located.

Liam used his flashing red lights to get them to the hospital as quickly as possible. No sirens—probably in deference to Micah.

"Did we get a name on this perp?" Garrett asked.

"Sam Lawrence." Liam glanced at him. "He showed up with the gunshot wound, very weak from blood loss. I'm convinced he's the one who got away in Volver County."

"Oh, yeah." He was amazed the guy had come in for

care. Then again, nearly dying tends to put things in perspective. "I hope he knows more that will point the finger at Edward Woodward. I can't shake the feeling he's the one responsible."

"If Jeremy makes it, we can work on convincing him to cooperate, too." Liam's expression turned thoughtful. "In fact, maybe I should call Edward to let him know his son has been shot."

"Don't you need to validate his ID first?" Liz asked.

Liam shrugged. "I could. But even if we don't know for sure, I might ask him to come verify the guy's ID. That gets Edward here in Wisconsin."

"I like that idea." Garrett wondered if Robert had been informed of Rebecca's death or if the rest of the family was keeping him in the dark on purpose.

He leaned toward the latter.

"We also need to find a way to speak to Robert directly." He glanced back at his son. "At the very least, he should know about Micah before he dies."

"Right after we hear what Sam Lawrence has to say." Liam grinned. "The hospital is up ahead."

"I see it." Liam had gotten them there in record time without being reckless. Garrett sat forward, eager to jump out of the vehicle the moment Liam had parked near the front entrance.

He grabbed the baby carrier, glancing at Liz. "I may need you to stay in the hallway with Micah."

Her brow furrowed, but she nodded. "If you think it's safe."

She had a point. He'd never taken a baby into a perp interview, but he wasn't willing to let anything happen to either Liz or Micah. Besides, it might be better for Liam to conduct the interview. "Okay, let's go."

Liam flashed his badge to the hospital staff. They were soon escorted to Sam Lawrence's room, where Abby stood on guard.

"Abernathy's lawyer just arrived," she said. "When you're done here, you should come down the hall to his room. I suspect he'll be ready to talk, too."

"I can't wait," Liam drawled. He entered the room and quickly introduced himself. Then he read Sam Lawrence his rights. "Do you understand your rights as I've described them to you?" Liam asked. "Are you willing to speak with me?"

"Yes." The man grimaced, putting a hand to his abdominal wound. "I'm not going down for this alone. You gotta give me less jail time, though."

"That can be arranged if we can verify your story." Liam got straight to the point. "Who hired you?"

"Edward Woodward."

"And who was your target?"

"I was hired to eliminate the cop, the nurse and the kid." He grimaced and shifted in the bed. "But I know there were other guys who were hired to take out Joel Abernathy."

The information clarified why Abernathy had been shot outside the meeting spot where he was to exchange Micah for cash.

"Who shot Rebecca Woodward?" Liam asked.

"Not me," the guy claimed.

"Who?" Liam pressed. His phone dinged with an incoming text, but he barely glanced at it. "You need to give us more if you expect to do less jail time."

"My partner. Kyle Gall." Sam's voice turned whiny. "I was there, but he shot her. Then we followed the nurse and the baby to Green Lake to try to finish the job."

Since Kyle Gall was likely dead, the only evidence they'd

have were the shell casings found at the parking lot outside their headquarters. "How did Rebecca's dead body end up at my place?" he asked.

Sam's eyes widened. "What? That's creepy! I had nothing to do with moving a dead body."

Oddly, Garrett believed him. They had what they needed to prove Edward was behind the shootings, but they still had to talk to Abernathy.

"You'll need to testify against Edward if you want less jail time," Liam said. "And we need proof that money exchanged hands."

"He paid me twenty grand, with another twenty once they were dead," Sam said. "And I secretly recorded the conversation as extra insurance in case he decided not to pay."

Garrett hated to admit he was impressed with the perp's cunning. One down, one more to talk to. He left the room, still carrying Micah. Liam fell into step beside him as Abby led the way to Abernathy's room. When Micah started to fuss, Liz quickly took the baby into her arms.

"I'll feed him." She offered a wan smile. "But I want to listen in."

He nodded and pulled a chair from the nurses' station so she could sit outside the door. Again, he let Liam take the lead. His boss scrolled through his phone for a moment, then nodded in satisfaction.

Liam approached Abernathy's bed. "I'm Sheriff Harland. I heard you're willing to make a statement?"

"Uh, yes." The way Abernathy's gaze darted to his lawyer made Garrett suspicious. "I believe my wife's uncle killed her, then tried to kill me and our son. I only approached Garrett because I wanted to keep my son safe."

"You'll take a DNA test?" Liam asked.

"I don't need to. Rebecca and I are—*were* legally married."

"No, see, I don't think so." Liam stepped closer. "Do you have proof?"

"Yes. I have my—*our* marriage certificate." Abernathy's gaze darted to his lawyer again. "I was desperate to get my son back. I acted out of extreme emotional distress."

His answers had been well coached. Too bad Garrett didn't believe him. Liam pressed on. "Do you have anything else? Like pictures of the happy occasion?"

"No. I—uh, Rebecca had them on her phone camera." Abernathy tilted his chin. "That's my statement. As soon as I'm medically cleared, I'll be taking my son home."

"No, you won't." Liam smiled without humor. He lifted up his phone. "My deputy just received Rebecca's phone records, and there are no photos of a wedding. In fact, there are plenty of text messages between the two of you that indicate she'd broken things off." Liam took another step forward, lowering his voice. "We'll prove the marriage certificate is fake, and a DNA test will prove Garrett Nichols is Micah's father. You're done, Abernathy. You might want to chat with your lawyer again, because as far as I'm concerned, forgery, attempted murder and attempted child abduction are just the initial charges on the table. Once we finish our investigation, more will follow."

For a long moment, Abernathy simply stared at him. Then his bravado collapsed like a popped balloon. "Okay, okay! I knew the kid wasn't mine."

"Stop talking!" his lawyer shouted. "Just stop!"

Abernathy fell silent, a sulky expression his face. Garrett knew it was over. There was no way he could talk himself out of this one. Turning, he joined Liz and Micah in the hallway.

"You got him," Liz murmured. "I'm so glad."

"Me, too. Those phone records sealed the deal." He

stroked Micah's downy hair. "We have both of them. Abernathy and Edward Woodward."

"Thank the Lord," she whispered. "God was really watching over us today."

"He was." Garrett ached to kiss her again, but a woman pushing a large red cart full of emergency supplies rushed past them. "We need to get out of here."

"Wyatt and I can drive you back to headquarters," Abby offered.

"I'd rather stay and help Liam," Wyatt said. He tossed his wife a key fob. "You go."

"And what will you be doing?" Abby asked.

"Based on this new statement, we'll call the Chicago PD to arrest Edward. Then I'll give him the news about his son being shot." Wyatt grinned. "I can hardly wait."

Garrett was confident Liam and Wyatt could handle this without him. "When Micah is finished, we'll hit the road."

"When can I return to my clinic?" Liz asked.

Her words were like a punch to the gut. He wasn't ready for her to leave. Yet, obviously, there were pregnant women who needed her.

"Only once we know for sure the danger is over." He forced a smile. "Shouldn't be too long. Once the news of Edward's arrest goes out, any lingering gunmen will likely scatter like cockroaches in the sunlight."

"I hope so," she murmured. "I'm ready for this to be over."

The danger? Or their time together? He was afraid to ask.

Abby didn't use red lights on the ride home, so it took longer. Sitting in the passenger seat, Garrett mulled over the best way to approach his feelings for Liz.

When Abby's phone rang, she used the hands-free functionality to answer. "Hey, Liam."

"Edward Woodward is in custody, and the local cops are

bringing him here to see his son." Liam's tone rang with satisfaction. "After you drop off Garrett and Liz, go to our headquarters. After his visit, I plan to question Edward. Not that I expect him to say much."

"Good," Abby responded with a grin. "Meet you there."

Normally, Garrett would want to be included. But not now, with his future happiness hanging in the balance.

What if Green Bay wasn't hiring? How close was Appleton or Oshkosh to Liz's clinic? He knew Cash Rawson had recently joined the Appleton Police Department, so he wasn't sure they were hiring.

By the time Abby pulled into the parking lot of their headquarters, he still wasn't sure what his future held.

He carried Micah to his office with Liz beside him. He set the baby carrier on his desk as Liz sank into the closest chair. He turned to face her. "I have something to tell you."

Liz tipped her head to the side, tucking a strand of her long dark hair behind her ear. "I'm listening."

Flowery words weren't his strong suit. He pulled the second desk chair over so he could sit close enough to take her hand. "We haven't known each other long, and this may sound sudden, but I've fallen in love with you."

Her eyes widened in surprise, but then a hint of wariness filled them. "Are you sure you're not just saying that because you need a mother for Micah?"

"You have been like a mother to him, but that's not what this is about." He held her gaze, imploring her to believe him. "When those gunmen had us trapped in the SUV, I thought our time on this earth was over. My biggest regret was not telling you about my feelings. I can handle Micah on my own, but I can't face a life without you, Liz. I know you live far away, and I'm willing to relocate."

"Relocate?" She looked confused. "To where?"

"Anywhere that will hire me." He bent to kiss her hand. "Please, Liz, give me a chance. I don't want to lose you."

"You would give up your career here to take a position closer to me?" She looked shocked.

"Yes. My life is more than my job. It's about having a family." He managed a crooked smile. "With you."

She sat silent for a long moment. So long that he feared she was looking for a way to let him down gently. Then she said, "I'm glad to hear this because I love you, too, Garrett."

A wave of relief washed over him. He stood and pulled her into his arms. "You've made me a happy man, Liz."

She laughed softly, then lifted up on her tiptoes to kiss him.

When they both needed to breathe, he broke off the kiss but gazed down at her. "I'll start applying for new jobs right away."

"There's no need for that, Garrett. I'll see if I can shift my newer patients to another OB and finish up with those who are due in the next few months."

He frowned. "I want you to be happy, Liz. I admire your dedication to serving the women on the reservation. I will be happy no matter where I end up."

"Most of my patients come from outside the reservation—and don't worry. We'll find a way to make it work."

"Yes, all that matters is that we love each other enough to make the effort." He still planned to apply for other jobs, but since it may take time, they'd have to compromise a bit. "I love you."

"I love you, too." She kissed him again, but then Micah began to fuss. He picked up his son, then pulled Liz into a three-way embrace.

He was truly blessed by the family God had given to him. A blessing he would never take for granted.

EPILOGUE

One week later...

Liz only delivered one baby after she was able to return to her clinic, so she spent her time seeking midwife support in covering her clinic. One woman in particular had expressed keen interest in taking over.

It was a big relief. As much as she'd loved caring for these women, she wasn't interested in staying out here alone any longer, though she had agreed to back up the new midwife as needed.

She and Garrett had taken Micah to a pediatrician, who pronounced him healthy and fit. She was glad the traumatic incident hadn't seemed to impact him.

Garrett called when she'd crossed into Green Lake County. Her rental car offered the hands-free functionality, so she used it now. "Hey, where are you?"

"About five minutes out, why?" She imagined him holding his son.

"Robert Woodward wants to talk. I'm setting up a video chat with him, and I'd like you to be with me."

Rebecca's father was still alive? Edward Woodward was in custody, and Liam was working with the Chicago PD to arrange for transport back to Illinois, where the initial murder for hire interaction had taken place. Rebecca's uncle had refused to talk, but the rest of the men in custody—including his son, Jeremy—were happy to place the blame squarely on Edward's shoulders. "I'll be there soon."

"Sounds good. Love you."

As always, his low, husky words made her smile. "Love you, too."

Garrett had had professional cleaners scour his house from top to bottom and had insisted on paying for the same treatment to Abby and Wyatt's house. Rebecca's phone records had proven her intent to break things off with Joel Abernathy, which had sent him into desperation mode to get custody of Micah.

Since the day Edward's arrest hit the news, everything had been quiet. No more strange gunmen had shown up in Green Lake or at her clinic. Obviously, anyone still lurking out there knew the likelihood of being paid the balance of their fee was zero to none. That, and they were likely hiding to avoid being prosecuted.

A fact that suited her just fine.

She pulled into Garrett's driveway, then hurried inside. Holding Micah, he crossed over to greet her with a kiss. "We missed you," he whispered.

"Same," she agreed. "What time is the call?"

He led her to the kitchen table, where he had his computer set up. "Now. Take a seat beside me."

She did as he asked, waiting as Garrett made the call. Less than a minute later, a pale, thin older man's face filled the screen.

"Garrett Nichols?" the man asked in a weak voice.

"Yes, sir. And this is your grandson, Micah." Garrett held the baby close to the screen.

Tears glittered in the sick man's eyes. "He's beautiful."

"Yes, he is. And this is midwife Liz Templeton. She delivered Micah and tried to save Rebecca's life."

"Nice to meet you," Robert said. "Thank you for being there for my daughter and for saving my grandson's life."

"You're welcome. But it was Garrett who kept him safe from Edward's gunmen," she added bluntly.

A pained expression crossed his features. "Yes, I know. I'm horrified about what transpired. But at least the Woodward fortune has an heir in Micah."

"No, sir, I don't want it." It was Garrett's turn to be blunt. "I'm sorry, but I respectfully ask that you change your will so that Micah is no longer a target."

A spark of anger flashed in Robert's eyes, but then he looked weary. "I understand your concern. It's not as if he can spend the money now, anyway. But Micah is a Woodward and deserves his inheritance."

"Please don't do this," she begged. "We barely escaped with our lives. If you truly love your grandson, you'll do as Garrett requested. Change your will to leave Micah out of it."

The older man was silent for a long moment. Then he said, "I do love my grandson. And I regret that I'll never get the chance to watch him grow up. Can I at least provide a college fund for him?"

When Garrett glanced at her, she gave a slight nod. "Yes, that would be nice," he said. "But set it up so that it covers other expenses, in case he decides not to attend a four-year university. I want Micah to do whatever he wants, even if that's a trade like being a plumber or an electrician." He smiled. "Even a cop."

Robert sighed. "I can do that. This puts me in a tough situation, though. The only people I can trust to take over the company is my sister, Connie, and her daughter, Anita."

Better them than Micah. But Liz held her tongue.

"There's one more thing," Garrett said. "Liz runs a clinic for low-income mothers. I would humbly request you provide a donation so that other pregnant women have the ability to get the care they need, just like Rebecca did."

"Done." Now there was a gleam in the older man's eyes. "I like that idea. I'll set aside ten million to start. I know that is what Rebecca would have wanted."

Ten million? She worked hard not to show the shock on her face. "Thank you, sir. That's very generous."

"I want to see my grandson in person," Robert said wistfully. "I'll get my lawyer here to change the will, but I would also like to send a private jet out to pick you up. I...don't know how much time I have left. I grow more and more weak each day."

"Of course," Garrett readily agreed. "But we can drive. No need for a private plane."

"I insist," Robert said. "Please? I want to hold him in my arms before I take my last breath."

Garrett glanced at her again, and she shrugged. Who was she to deny the wishes of a dying man?

"Okay," Garrett conceded. "That will be fine. Thank you, again."

"See you soon." Robert's voice trailed off and he looked away, his eyes drifting closed as if the brief interaction had sapped his strength.

When Garrett disconnected from the call, she asked, "Why didn't you warn me about the donation?"

He smiled. "I wanted to surprise you. I had a feeling he'd go along with the plan."

She leaned forward and kissed him. "You're a sneaky one. And I have news, too. I found another midwife to take over my clinic. With the additional funds from Robert's donation, I think I can get another midwife or two on staff, too. They can expand the clinic, maybe even relocate it so that they can provide care to a broader base of patients." She searched his gaze, then added, "I want to live here in Green Lake with you, Garrett."

"Are you asking me to marry you?" he teased.

"No!" Her cheeks burned with embarrassment. "I just realized I don't want to stay in the clinic anymore. It was exactly what I needed after losing Willow, but now?" She shook her head helplessly. "I loved meeting Wyatt, Abby and Liam. You have a wonderful community here. And I'd like to be a part of it."

"I'm thrilled to hear that." He smiled and pulled a ring box from his pocket. "I planned to wait for us to have a romantic dinner before asking you this, but this seems to be the perfect moment. Lizbeth, will you please marry me?"

She wrapped her arms around him and hugged him close. "Yes, Garrett. I'd be honored to be your wife."

"I love you." He kissed her, and she clung to him for a moment before breaking off to kiss Micah.

"I love both the men in my life." She rested a hand on Micah's back. She couldn't have loved the baby any more than if she'd given birth to him herself. She would always have a small hole in her heart for Willow, but now she couldn't wait to find out what God had in store for her, Garrett and Micah.

Her family.

* * * * *

Dear Reader,

I hope you've enjoyed the final book set in beautiful Green Lake, Wisconsin. I really enjoyed writing Garrett and Liz's story, and I will miss the characters who have made their homes in this wonderful town.

I am currently plotting my next book but no spoilers here. You'll just have to be patient to hear what's coming next.

I adore hearing from my readers! I can be found through my website at https://www.laurascottbooks.com, via Facebook at https://www.facebook.com/LauraScottBooks, Instagram at https://www.instagram.com/laurascottbooks/, and Twitter https://twitter.com/laurascottbooks. Also, take a moment to sign up for my monthly newsletter to learn about my new book releases. (I promise I'll keep you informed about my next project!) All subscribers receive a free novella not available for purchase on any platform.

Until next time,
Laura Scott